"T

AND

SCREENSHOTS"

By

Necie Holland

Acknowledgments:

First and foremost, I would like to thank the Almighty which from whom all my blessings flow. My parents, Angela Bryson and Charles Holland, for giving me this gift. I wouldn't be here and none of this would be possible if it weren't for you guys. I love you both dearly. To my son, Nyshuan, my brother, Anthony Stewart and sister, Sha'Cora Pickens, everything I do is for you guys and this is only the beginning for us! A special thank you to my best friend, Jasmine Sloan for always believing in me and being my backbone when I didn't have one of my own. To Cole Hart and the ENTIRE BankRoll Squad and TBRS team, I graciously thank you all for taking a chance on a small town country girl like myself! I pray that this is the start of something great that we can all eat GOOD off of!! Thank you all for the support thus far!

XOXOXOXO-

Necie "Ms.Write" Holland

"THUGS THOTS AND SCREENSHOTS"

Charese would have never thought that her life would come crashing down around her, that everything would fall apart right before her very eyes. Hell, she was what most niggas would call a bad bitch. She made sure that all of her shit was official and well put together. She was one of the most popular dancers at the club she worked at, Club Fantasy. She was Charese or Reesy to her friends and family, but known as Moet by the club patrons. She was bad, at least in her eyes. You couldn't tell her shit. She was beautiful and she knew it. She stood at 5'5; she was one hundred and forty five pounds, thick thighs, and perky 34C cups, long, jet-black hair, a fat ass, and blemish free mocha chocolate skin.

She shouldn't have even been at the club, but everyone falls on hard times. She just wanted to get her money right and live her dreams. Her dream was to own a hair salon. She reached her goal; she just wished she didn't have to go through the things she went through to get there. She was trying to rush through traffic so that she could make it back to the salon on time. It was four fifteen and she was already running behind because she had a four thirty appointment. She was at a red light when she turned and locked eyes with Bryce. Bryce Westland... the man that used to make her pussy tingle and her panties wet from thinking of him alone. She looked away and thanked God the light turned green. She thought back to when they used to kick it, back before shit changed...

Chapter 1

FIVE YEARS PRIOR

"Reesy! Reesy!"

She turned around to see Bryce rushing through the crowd to catch up to her. He stopped when he caught up to her and smiled. "What's up girl?" he asked.

"Nothing," she replied as they hugged.

"Where you headed?" he asked as they reached her '03 Nissan Altima.

"School," she answered.

"So when you gonna let me take you out?" he asked as he opened her car door for her then shut it.

"One day, maybe," was her reply.

She started her engine and pulled off. He had been trying to get with her since she was in the eleventh grade at Westside High School. She had since graduated and was pursuing a cosmetology license. She lived with her Aunt Kathy and her husband Charles. She had been with them since she was twelve when her mom died from Aids. Her father was strung out on heroin when she passed and was living on the street, so she and her older brother had no choice but to move in with their aunt. Her father overdosed two years after her mother passed, and her brother was murdered three days after her father's death, in a drug deal gone wrong.

She hated living with her aunt and uncle but she didn't have any other choice. Aunt Kathy did nothing but sit on the phone and gossip all day and Uncle Charles was a grumpy old man that was mad at the world, because he had lost a leg and was on disability. They lived in a rundown house on the Southside of Anderson, South Carolina. Los Anderson was what they called it. She lived on Spencer Street, which was considered the rough part of the neighborhood. It was always littered with junkies and ladies of the night. She was hell bent on getting on her feet and getting her own place outside of Anderson. She was trying to get money.

She pulled up at school and found a parking space then grabbed her bag and reapplied her lip-gloss before headed inside the building. Upon entering, she was immediately greeted by her best friend Courtni. Courtni was the same age as she was, nineteen. She was light-skinned, stood at about 5'8, and was very skinny. She probably weighed one hundred pounds soaking wet. But she was the closest thing Charese had to a sister.

"What's up girl?" she asked Charese as she was setting up her station.

"Ready to be done with this shit!" Charese replied, referring to school. They both shared a laugh.

Her body language suddenly changed and Charese followed her ice-cold stare to see what the cause was. Courtni had her eyes glued on Toya. They both hated that bitch. She thought she was hot shit but she stole most of the designer clothes that she rocked, and the rest she got because she was Kane's girlfriend. You couldn't tell her she wasn't bad, but Charese thought otherwise. You must believe that Charese wasn't hating. She spoke real shit only. Toya was about 4'11, and a real yellow bone, like Lisa Raye's complexion.

She wasn't bad looking, but she had a bad case of acne and an overbite with bucked teeth. Charese could admit that Toya had a shape that would make even Beyoncé look twice, but that's all she had going for herself. With all the time and maintenance she spent on shoes and clothes, you would think she could do better than some nappy track pieces slapped on top of her head. You could always see the tracks showing because she didn't have enough hair to cover them up.

Charese didn't see what Kane saw in her. Now Kane? Kane was that nigga. He owned this little strip club off Clemson Boulevard called Club Fantasy. He had stacks on top of stacks and only niggas that were getting money fucked with his club. Kane was sexy as hell. He was about 6'4", had a peanut butter complexion, rocked a low cut that had the deepest waves and was always lined up right, as was the goatee he sported, and he was about 250 pounds of solid muscle. He was as cut as a body builder. He had many cars, even more houses, and a lot of bitches. A lot of niggas respected him, but mainly because they were always kissing his ass. He had been trying to "recruit" Charese for the longest, but there was no way she would ever stoop that low.

Kane made those girls do any and everything.

Now Toya, she didn't dance, she was just the head bitch in charge. Charese and Courtni watched as Toya walked over to a girl in their class and grabbed her by her hair.

"Bitch, where is Kane's money?" she asked through clenched teeth.

Caught completely off guard, the girl began to stutter.

"I - I'm trying to get it now Toya," said the visibly frightened girl.

"That ain't good enough. If he doesn't get paid then I don't get paid and I take that personal," Toya said as she tightened her grip on the girl's hair. She handed her a small baggie.

"Be at the club tonight by ten. You owe me, not Kane, so you're going to work your debt off. And make sure you use all of that," she said referring to the cocaine that was inside the baggie.

"I don't do that anymore," the girl said as she began to cry.

"You raggedy little bitch. You're going to learn to do as you're told," Toya said, threw with the conversation. She let her hair go then turned to leave, but not before yelling "don't make me come back!"

Chapter 2

A week had passed since that little episode with the girl from school and Charese hadn't seen her since. Charese was thinking about her as she rode with Bryce to IHOP. She decided to finally let him take her out. They arrived at IHOP and were seated upon thirty minutes of waiting. As they were being seated, Charese couldn't help but notice Kane with some of his girls. She watched one girl cut up his pancakes while another tucked his napkin into his shirt.

Reading her mind Bryce said, "Promise me that will never be you."

"Never," Charese promised.

"Good. I'd take care of you before I let you shake your ass for that nigga."

She laughed. "And how you gonna do that?"

"Oh, you got jokes?" he asked. "I'm serious though. I'm gonna wife you one day."

"Whatever," she brushed him off as their food arrived.

She felt someone staring at her. She looked up and locked eyes with Kane. He winked at her and it made her sick to her stomach. Halfway through their meal, Kane walked up with a girl on each arm. He completely ignored

Bryce sitting next to Charese and said, "The beautiful Miss Charese Shaw... and how are you?"

"She good homeboy," Bryce said.

Kane gave him an evil look and he returned it. He wasn't intimidated like most niggas in Anderson were and Charese respected that. Kane broke the stare and returned his attention to Charese.

"You look good as always," he said.

"Thank you," Bryce said while tilting his glass towards Kane. That time, both Kane and Charese looked at Bryce like he was crazy.

Kane snapped, "Nigga, who the fuck are you?" he asked.

"Bryce," he said as he stood up, "Nigga."

Charese thought she was about to piss on herself. She grabbed Bryce by the hand and pulled him back down to where she was still sitting, but he never broke eye contact with Kane.

"Charese, I'll holla at you," Kane said. He looked at Bryce then walked away. Bryce watched him until he was out of sight.

"Bryce, are you crazy!" Charese exclaimed.

"Only about you," was his response.

"I'm serious. Do you know who Kane is?"

"I know who that nigga is. Shit, do y'all know who the fuck I am?" Bryce shouted. Charese could tell he was getting mad.

"Yea, a nigga with a death wish!" Charese joked trying to lighten the mood, but Bryce didn't laugh.

"I'm gonna get that nigga. Watch," he threatened.

"What?" Charese asked, trying to make sure that she heard him right.

"Let's go," he said while grabbing her by the arm. They left without saying another word.

****

"Reesy, where you been girl? You act like you don't know nobody anymore," her cousin Porsche said.

"I know right. The bitch must've got ahold to some good dick," her sister Mercedes joked as they all laughed.

They were at the food court in the Anderson Mall. Charese was the first to recover.

"Nah, y'all know I be on my grind," she said to her cousins with a smile.

"Well, we wanted to meet up because we both have some news to share," Mercedes said. "I'll go first. I started working at Fantasy, but don't think any less of me okay?"

Charese almost choked on her food. "But why Mimi?" she asked.

"Because I got fired and you know Tonio works for Kane, so I'll be okay. It's really not that bad Reesy," she said.

Charese sucked her teeth, but didn't say anything. She couldn't stand Mimi's baby daddy. Tonio was a bum. He had Mimi living in Anderson Gardens where three of his other baby mamas lived. Technically, Anderson Gardens was its former name, it was now called Belton Woods, but if you were from Anderson then AG was always going to be AG. No matter what you renamed it, it was still the projects. Charese and Porsche were always having to go out there on some bullshit. Tonio had eleven kids and five baby mamas. Mimi had three with him. He used to try to get with Charese back in the day, but she saw straight through him so he started talking to her home girl instead and had twin girls with her.

Mercedes wasn't a bad looking woman although Porsche was the prettier sister. Mercedes was about 5'9, one hundred and ten pounds, she had no kind of shape whatsoever, and she was the spitting image of actress Terri J. Vaughn. Meanwhile, Porsche was the same height, but probably about twenty pounds heavier, and a shade lighter than Mimi's brown-skinned complexion. Porsche was often compared to Nia Long.

"So what's your news bitch?" Charese asked turning her attention to Porsche.

She wasted no time. "I'm pregnant," she said.

"Aww hell," Charese said clearly taken aback.

"And I'm about to start working at the club too," she finished.

Charese looked at her like she was crazy. "Does Justin know?" she asked.

Justin was Porsche's long time on again, off again boyfriend. He was ugly, but he was a good man and took very good care of her.

"No, because it's not his," she said while holding her head down.

Charese's mouth fell to her chest. "Wow" was all that she could say. They ate the rest of their food in silence. Charese got up, deciding to get some ice cream from Chick-Fil-A.

But first she had to ask, "So who's your baby daddy girl?"

"Kane," Porsche said barely above a whisper.

Charese threw her hands up in exasperation as she sat back down in her chair. "Aww hell!" she said.

Chapter Three

Three weeks had passed since Porsche dropped her bomb on Charese. There was about to be a whole lot of drama, but Charese wasn't going to let Toya fuck with her cousin. She had been playing on Porsche's phone and threatening her. Porsche screenshot every message and posted it on Facebook. Now all the bitches in the hood were choosing sides and all the niggas were waiting around anticipating the fight of the century. Charese was ready to fuck Toya up but she had yet to run into her. She hadn't seen her since she ran up in her school like she owned the building.

Charese was lying on the living room couch watching "The First 48." Uncle Charles was sitting at the kitchen table talking shit to Aunt Kathy as usual, and she was cursing him right back out. Charese always found it funny. She was in the middle of painting her toenails when she heard somebody knock at the door. She went to answer the door and was met by the finest man she had ever seen around her way.

"Can I help you?" she asked the stranger.

He hesitated for a moment before he answered. "Um, yea, my car broke down and my phone just died. I wanted to know if I could use your phone?"

"Sure," she said as she opened the door enough for him to come in.

"And this is kind of embarrassing, but can I use your bathroom?" he asked as he flashed a smile, a smile that caught Charese completely off guard. He had that beautiful Taye Diggs smile.

"It's straight through the back, last door on the right," she said. He headed towards the bathroom, speaking to her aunt and uncle along the way.

Her inquisitive aunt came running to the door, where she was still standing.

"Child, who is that fine ass man in my bathroom?" she asked.

"I don't know. His car broke down and he wanted to use the phone," Charese said as she pointed to his car that was still sitting in the middle of the street.

"You better get him," Aunt Kathy said and winked her eye at Charese. She walked back into the kitchen and handed him the phone as he was coming out of the bathroom. Upon completing his call, he returned to the living room.

"Thanks. I had to call my job and let them know that I would be late," he said with a smile.

"Oh," was all she could think of to say.

"Do you have jumper cables?"

"Yea," she said as she carefully slid her feet into her flip-flops.

Noticing her concern, the man said, "Oh, I'll take you to get them done shawty. It ain't no thang."

Damn. Signs of a thug nigga came out of him and it turned Charese on.

"My name Tee," he said.

"Charese," she replied. "Come on."

She led him to their cars, got his started, said goodbye to him then turned to walk away.

He stopped her. "Yo, baby girl, when you gonna let a nigga make it up to you?"

She told him that she would think about it and he left it at that. He stood there for a minute, then got into his car and left.

Charese heard her cell phone go off as she walked into the house. It was a picture message from Courtni. She looked at the message and shook her head. Screenshots could fuck up a relationship in the blink of an eye. Courtni caught her boyfriend cheating and the girl he cheated with screenshot all of his "I love you" messages. Charese called Courtni and she picked up on the first ring.

"Bitch, I'm pissed," Courtni hissed.

"Who is she?" Charese asked.

"Some girl named Florencia from the East side."

"Flo from Quarry Street?" Charese asked.

"Hell, I don't know," Courtni said dismissively."

"She inboxed me on Facebook so I gave her my number."

"Damn," Charese said.

"I'm ready to fuck all his shit up though! But what you doing girl?"

"Nothing, watching TV," Charese replied.

"Oh. Well, I'll be over there after I leave Tony's house," Courtni said.

"Be good Courtni," Charese warned. They hung up.

She looked for something to put on in the hall closet where she kept her clothes, took a shower, then bumped a few curls in her hair. After putting on her shoes she walked down the street to her homegirl, Tip's house. When she arrived, Tip answered in nothing but a towel on.

"What's up boo? Come in. I was just putting some clothes on," she said.

Tip was one of Charese's close friends. Her circle consisted of Courtni, Tip, and Taye. She wasn't as close to Tip and Taye as she was to Courtni, but they were still her girls. She and Tip had done some wild shit together in the past. They got drunk at a party and started kissing, which led to Tip laying Charese down and licking her clit with such gentleness and perfection that it left Charese feeling weak and confused. That night, Tip confessed to Charese that she was bisexual. She ate Charese's pussy so good that she didn't even care. They had been "bumping cooties" from time to time ever since. She would be lying to herself if she said she didn't like it. Charese watched Tip as she dressed.

Tip was in her bra and panties when Charese walked up to her from behind and started caressing her round 'D' cups. She turned to face Charese and they started kissing. She palmed her plump ass while Charese pulled her panties to the side and started rubbing her fingers against her warm womanhood. She was so wet that it immediately turned Charese on. She slipped two fingers inside Tip's moist slit causing her to moan, but stopped once Tip started taking her shorts off.

They didn't say a word to each other as they lay on opposite ends of the bed and connected to each other in a scissors-like position, with their pussies directly on top of one another. They bumped and rubbed until they both reached their climax. It felt so good. It was such an unexplainable feeling. Of course Charese loved dick, but she had a special love for pussy.

Tip was the only woman that she had ever been with. They ended their little session by taking a shower together. Charese put her clothes back on and Tip slipped into a sundress.

She looked so good in the dress that Charese said, "Alright now, you gonna make me take you back in that room!"

Tip laughed at her. "You want to go to the park?"

"Yea," Charese agreed.

Tip grabbed her keys, locked her door, and they headed to the park.

Chapter Four

Charese and Tip walked to the park and Charese couldn't help but admire Tip's beauty. Tip was 5'2, one hundred and thirty pounds, and thick in all the right places. She had a caramel complexion with long, thick hair with hues of brown and red that complemented her hazel eyes. Every nigga in Anderson County wanted Tip as much as they wanted Charese. They walked through the park and sat on a bench near the basketball court. They took notice to all the local thugs and dope boys engaging in a rowdy game of basketball, putting on for the sea of women that were walking around trying to be seen.

"These bitches some real live thots," Tip commented.

"Right," Charese agreed. "They're trying too hard."

"Hell, all I have to do is sit my pretty ass down and the niggas will come flocking," Tip boasted.

Charese was silent as they watched the game.

"There go ya boy," Tip finally said with a smirk on her face.

Charese scanned the crowd until she laid eyes on who Tip was referring to. Her ex-boyfriend, Trap, was running the ball up and down the court with his nasty ass. He cheated on her with a girl named Shi Shi who ended up

23

giving him an STD. He in turn, exposed Charese to it. Shi Shi stole Charese's number from Trap's phone, kept sending her pictures of her vagina and talking big shit, so Charese set her up. She told her that she was nasty for walking around burning people and Shi Shi's reply was "So what. Your man likes it." Charese screenshot the whole conversation and posted it on her Facebook page. She dumped Trap then promptly put her foot in Shi Shi's ass. Charese caught up with Shi Shi at Club Maui and beat her down in the parking lot. Charese was embarrassed that it happened to her, but thank God that it was something she could get rid of.

"Let's walk over there to that other picnic table," Tip suggested.

"Aight," Charese agreed. They got up and started walking past the basketball court.

"Damn, Tip, you looking good as usual," one dude said.

"What's up Reesy, with your sexy ass?" said another.

They both spoke and waved at the men as they walked by.

"Hey Reesy!"

She turned to see who was yelling her name and saw her homeboy, Jarron, running towards her. He caught up to them and had the nerve to put his sweaty arms around her.

"What's up with a hair do?" he asked.

"Anytime sexy, I'm on your time," she replied.

"You better stop Reesy, you gonna get me in trouble," he smiled.

"I know," she said, "I don't want to have to beat your girlfriend up."

His girlfriend, Maya, was a jealous bitch when it came to him. Charese had witnessed many fights involving Maya and other women.

"Come to the house tomorrow at three," she told him.

"You gonna be there Tip?" Jarron asked, flirting with Tip.

"Boy, shut up!" Tip said as she playfully smacked his arm.

"Well aight ladies. Let me get back to this game," Jarron said. He ran back to the basketball court.

Charese told Tip that she was walking up the street to the candy lady's house. That lady was getting off. She sold everything from *Now & Laters* to weed and hot dogs. Charese left with two cigars and a can soda. She already had weed. She got her weed from a nigga named Pick that had the Southside on lock. As she was crossing the street, she spotted Courtni. Courtni stopped her car in front of her.

"Bitch where you going and why you not answering your phone?" Courtni questioned.

Charese reached around herself and realized that she didn't have her phone on her.

"Aww shit, I must've left it at the house," she said. "We at the park chillin'. Come on."

She hopped in the car and rode back to the park with Courtni. They parked and walked towards the basketball court. When they reached the picnic table Tip was sitting and talking to Jarron and his friend. Charese sat down and started to roll a blunt.

"What y'all smoking on? Some midget?" Jarron asked.

"Bullshit!" Charese said as she held the bag up to his nose so that he could smell how good her loud smelled.

He pulled out his own bag and began rolling up. They all sat around blazing and laughing as they watched Courtni reenact her recent encounter with her cheating boyfriend. She trashed her boyfriend's apartment and then wrecked his car. Jarron ended up going to get some beer from the candy lady and they sat around and chilled well past eleven o' clock. Everyone left with Courtni dropping Charese and Tip off at their respective houses.

Charese grabbed her phone as soon as she walked inside and noticed that she had seven messages and five missed calls. She had two messages and three voicemails from Mekhi, a dude she spent time with sometimes. She laughed out loud as she erased his messages and hung up the phone. Mekhi meant absolutely nothing to her. He was a sucker. He wanted her so bad that he allowed her to walk all over him, which turned her off. She needed a nigga that was going to tell her to sit her ass down somewhere if she got out of hand. And for that reason, she only fucked with him on occasion. She fucked with him enough to get what she wanted out of him.

He was a good man. He came from a middle-class, two-parent home. He worked, he was pursuing a degree, attended church on Sundays, the whole nine. His money was long and he didn't mind spending it on her. Honest money was another thing that turned her off. She needed a thug; a hard ass nigga with a lot of swag; the type that would come home from a hard day out on the block, take his Timbs off and give her some of that dope dick. Damn, she was getting turned on just thinking about it.

She looked at a text message she received from Trap. He was begging her to take him back and apologizing for giving her an STD. She laughed out loud as she screenshot the message and posted to her Facebook page with a "check this nigga out" caption and some gunshot emojis.

I'm petty as hell, she said to herself as she laughed out loud.

She put her phone on the charger, took a shower then got ready for bed. Before she knew it she was sound asleep.

She overslept the next morning and got to class during the last forty-five minutes of its session.

"Bitch, you so stupid!" Courtni said as soon as she saw her and started laughing.

Charese feigned ignorance. "What?" she asked.

"Why you do that nigga like that?" Courtni asked while still laughing.

Charese had to laugh herself. "He knew better," she said.

They cut hair and cut up with each other for the remainder of class. After class, Charese was hungry so she went to Zaxby's. Deciding to eat in, she ordered her food then took a seat in a corner booth. All of sudden, Bryce popped up out of nowhere and took a seat next to her.

"What's up sexy?" he asked.

"Hey Bryce," she said with a smile. Charese had to admit to herself that he was kind of sexy.

"You look good today," he complimented her.

"Please," she said, waving her hand dismissively in the air. She had on an old Westside t-shirt from high school, some form fitting jeans, and some old navy flip-flops. Her hair was pulled up into a messy bun.

The cashier called his order. He went to retrieve his food and returned to his seat next to Charese. They laughed while they ate then he walked her to her car before going back to his job. Charese drove away and called Porsche. She picked up on the first ring.

"Hello," she answered.

"You home?" Charese asked.

"No at the room with Kane. He went to take care of something so I can talk for a minute."

"Porsche, what in the hell are you doing with him?" Charese exclaimed.

"Status girl!" Porsche laughed as if she said something funny. "I wasn't planning on getting pregnant by the nigga!"

"Toya still fuckin with you?" Charese asked.

"Nah, she knows better! I ain't worried about her," Porsche said.

29

"Well bitch, good luck with that. I gotta go. Bye," Charese said as she hung up the phone on Porsche. She had to be short with her cousin because it pissed her off when women couldn't appreciate a good man. Justin was good to Porsche. Meanwhile, she was always attracting the dogs and male whores.

She was driving, going nowhere in particular, just enjoying the sun. She wasn't aware of her surroundings until she realized she was damn near in Belton, a neighboring small town. She took a right turn on to Howard Lane and headed to AG to see Mimi.

Chapter Five

Taniko Harris aka Tee was feeling good. He was new to Anderson. It was a little city and a little too laid back for his taste, but it was growing on him. It amazed him how the ladies kept throwing themselves at him; all except for one. The little lady that helped him out when his car broke down. *What was her name?* he asked himself. Charese. Yea that was it. Now that bitch was sexy! A fine little chocolate chic. He wasn't bad looking himself. He stood about 6'1, two hundred and twenty pounds, his dreads were long with red tips that fell to the middle of his back, and he had a deep chocolate complexion. He was midnight dark.

A promotion at his job in Columbia caused him to move to Anderson. He started messing with a girl that went crazy after he fucked her and dropped her. He wasn't even at his job a full month before she got him fired. Now he was stuck working at Electrolux, a refrigerator company, for close to nothing. But hey, whatever paid the bills. He was chilling in the parking lot of an apartment complex with a dude named Vic from work. They were hanging around a couple of other men that Tee didn't know.

"Nigga, drink that shit and stop playing with it!" Vic said referring to the cup of liquor that Tee had been holding.

"Chill out nigga, I got this," Tee said.

The door to the apartment they were in front of, opened and a woman stepped out to take a bag of trash to the dumpster, which was adjacent to the building. She wasn't really his type, but for some reason she reminded him of Charese.

"Aww man," Vic said when he noticed Tee looking at the woman. "Don't even waste your time bruh. That's Mimi, one of Tonio's bitches." All of the other dudes started laughing.

"Man, I wasn't sweatin' her, she just looks like somebody," Tee said.

Just then, a car came out of nowhere blasting loud music.

If it ain't about money don't be blowin' me up nigga I ain't gettin up. If it ain't about money.

The car parked beside them. Tee watched intensely as Charese got out.. He had recognized the car as soon as she pulled up. She got out as Mimi was walking back from her trip to the dumpster. Charese didn't even look their way as she sat on the hood of her car.

"What's up bitch!" Mimi yelled as she walked towards the car.

Tee looked Charese up and down in lust. She had on a t-shirt, some tight jeans that fit her hips just right, and some flip-flops. It looked like she hadn't combed her hair, but to Tee she still looked good.

"Nothing bitch, just came from Zaxby's and ended up over here. You see I don't have any clothes on," Charese said as she tugged at her clothes.

"Aye, what's up Reesy?" a man sitting beside Vic yelled. "When you gonna stop being stuck up and come spend the night with me with your thick ass?"

She looked in their direction and stuck her middle finger up. Her frown turned into a smile when she spotted Tee.

He threw his arms up in the air. "When we goin' baby girl? I'm waiting on you!" he said.

"Hey Tee," she said as she blushed.

All of the men, including Vic, looked at him in disbelief.

"Pick ya mouth up nigga," he said as he smirked at Vic and made his way over to Charese.

He gave her a hug, and surprisingly, she returned it. Mimi was staring just as hard as Vic and his friends were. He extended his hand and introduced himself to Mimi.

"What's up? I'm Tee," he said flashing that beautiful Taye Diggs smile.

"Mercedes," she said as she took his hand.

He turned his attention back to Charese and looked down at her feet.

"I see you still need them feet done," he stated.

Mimi's eyes were bulging out of her head but Charese didn't even notice. She forgot that Mimi was even standing there. She was too focused on the nigga standing in front of her. She finally found her voice.

"Nah, you don't have to do that," she said.

"I told you it ain't no thang," he insisted.

"Alright, let's go," she said calling his bluff.

"Come on," he said. He shook Mimi's hand again, "Nice meeting you."

It was then that Charese noticed that her cousin was still standing there.

"I'll be back," she said to Mimi. Mimi just looked at her.

"Aye, I'll catch up to you later," Tee hollered over at Tank. All of the niggas started tripping and talking shit.

And with that, Tee and Charese were gone.

Chapter Six

"Yo Bryce, let's go to Wendy's," Champ was saying.

Bryce Westland paid him no attention. He was concentrating on his supply that he was cutting up. They were in Belton at Champ's sister apartment in Oak Forest. Bryce was a dope boy, but few people knew. He wasn't the thugged out type like the rest. Not to be deceived by his looks, Bryce was no pushover. He was low-key in every move he made. He was about 5'9, brown skinned and about one hundred and eighty pounds.

He drove a 08' Altima and didn't stunt like he had money, nor was his wardrobe up to par. He was cool with a white tee and some jeans. He had a little job at Advance Auto Parts, but that was just for show. Bitches weren't throwing themselves at him and he was perfectly fine with that. He preferred it that way. He wasn't about to spend all of his hard earned money on any of these Los Anderson thots. He always had his eyes on Charese Shaw; she was pure beauty.

He had a little paper and a couple of trap houses, but he kept all of his valuable possessions at his cousin's house in Greenwood, which was about an hour away. He gave his cousin a couple of hundreds every month and paid her bills to ensure the safekeeping of his things. No one knew he was even on the radar because they didn't see him balling out of control in that bullshit Club Fantasy. Yes, he had been there before. Some bullshit had happened a while back so he ain't fuck with Kane or his strip club. He was just trying to stack his paper so that when he was ready to take over he could step to Charese and she would take him seriously. He was going to set her up right.

He had a lot of things on his mind so he rode to Wendy's with Champ in silence. Champ was his right hand man. Nobody fucked with Champ because he was known for leaving body parts lying around. That crazy fool hailed from East Atlanta. Bryce's team consisted of himself, Champ, Dub, Seven, and his cousin Kat. His squad was tight, and they were strong. They arrived back from Wendy's and sat down at the table to eat.

"I ain't tell you I saw that nigga Kane at IHOP a minute ago?" Bryce stated.

"What!" Champ said in between chicken nuggets. "Say word?"

"Word my nigga, but check this out, that nigga don't even remember me bruh. Now you supposed to be that nigga right? But you don't remember the face of ya enemies?" he said.

"I remember every face," Champ said, "Every face."

"Hell yea," Bryce continued, "Now this nigga should have lost his life that night and you don't even remember the face of the man that almost took it from you?"

"Word my nigga," Champ said in agreement, as he finished his meal.

"Shit, I even told that nigga who I was. Ya feel me bruh?"

They finished eating and went back to work. Bryce sold everything: hard, soft, green, meth, and pills. By the time Bryce looked up, they had been working for three hours. He was tired.

"Yo bruh, I'm about to take two bricks back to my spot. I want you to bag up half of this for me and you can keep the rest," he said.

"Aight," Champ said.

"Call Kat and tell him to help you move that soft and I'll catch up to y'all later," Bryce said.

They dapped each other up and Bryce headed out the door into the cold February night.

Chapter Seven

Charese walked into the house and flopped down on the couch. She had just come home from another date with Tee. They had a blast and she really got to know him. He showed her pictures of his three-year-old daughter. She was shocked that he had a child, but even more shocked to learn that he was twenty-seven. The oldest she had ever dated was twenty-one to her eighteen, now here he was eight years her senior. Her phone rang and she was not surprised when his name flashed across the screen. Normally she would have been annoyed at his persistence, but she was actually flattered.

"Hey you," she said as she answered.

"What's up? I just wanted to make sure you made it home," he said.

"Yep, I'm about to shower and go to bed," she said.

"So early?" he teased.

"Now you know I have to get up early," she said.

"Yeah that is right, you do have somebody's scalp to burn," he teased her again. They shared a laugh.

"Well sweet dreams boo," he said.

They said their goodnights and hung up the phone. She took a quick shower and went to bed. The next day she woke up with Tee on her mind. She was really feeling him. She got dressed in some black leggings, a white wife beater, and some Adidas. She twisted her hair up, curled it, then walked out the door.

Upon arriving at school, she was met in the parking lot by Courtni who had a sad look on her face.

"What's wrong with you bitch?" she asked her best friend as she approached her.

"Your house phone has been busy all night, your cell was off, and we've been trying to reach you! Where were you? Everybody has been calling! Oh my gosh!" Courtni frantically said. She started crying and that scared the hell out of Charese.

She grabbed Courtni by her shoulders and started shaking her. "Tell me what's wrong!" she demanded. She was not prepared for what Courtni said next.

"Porsche's in the hospital, they don't think she's going to make it," she said. She had to jump to grab Charese before she hit the ground.

"What happened?" asked a hysterical Charese.

"She got jumped at the club last night. Toya set her up. Girl, did you know she was pregnant by Kane?"

"Oh Lord," was all Charese could say.

"Come on. Let's go," Courtni said while grabbing Charese by her hand and leading her to her car.

Charese prayed the entire way to the hospital. When they arrived at the room Mimi was there holding her sister's hand. When she saw Charese, she ran to her and they hugged each other tight.

"Oh Reesy, I was there, I should have done something!" Mimi cried.

Charese looked over at Porsche. Both of her eyes were swollen, one completely shut. She had bandages around her head, a neck brace, and a shoulder sling.

"I swear I'm going to kill those bitches!" Mimi said while looking at her sister. "She's in critical condition. They can't stop the internal bleeding. They don't think she's going to make it!"

Mimi was hysterical. They sat her in a chair and tried to calm her down.

"Mimi what happened?" Charese asked through fresh tears.

Mimi told them how Toya and a stripper named Tasty beat her baby sister unconscious, stabbed her multiple times, and left her for dead. A security guard found her in one of the private rooms and got her some help. Porsche started stirring in her sleep and they all ran to her side.

Chapter Eight

"Mimi do you have your purple stilettos with you tonight?" Porsche asked her sister.

"Yeah," Mimi said as she handed her the heels.

"Bitch I'm getting fucked up tonight," a stripper named Tasty said.

"And it's some ballers out there too," said another dancer.

"Hell yea," Tasty agreed as they hi-fived each other.

"I'm about to go get me a dance," the stripper said as she got up to leave. She walked past a nervous Porsche who was still putting on her shoes.

"So you're new right?" Tasty asked her.

"Yeah, call me Wet Wet," Porsche said with a smile.

"Aye Buttah, you wanna powder your nose before you go out?" a dancer said to Mimi calling her by her stage name.

"Yea," Mimi replied.

Porsche looked at her sister in disbelief. She grabbed her arm as she was walking away.

"Bitch, are you crazy? I know you're not sniffin' no powder!" Porsche exclaimed.

43

"Bitch, will you mind your business?" Mimi said as she jerked her arm away and walked over to the group of girls that were huddled in a corner around the girl with the bag. Mimi grabbed the bag, stuck the dollar bill in it, and sucked the white substance up through her nose. Porsche couldn't take watching anymore.

"I gotta get out of here," she said more to herself than to Tasty, who seemed to be stuck up under her.

"I'm right behind you," Tasty said as they both left the room.

The club is packed tonight, Porsche thought to herself. She spotted a man sitting in a corner by himself and started walking in his direction but someone pushed her into a room and she fell head first on the floor.

"Got dammit!" Porsche screamed and she got up and turned around. Tasty was locking the door.

"Bitch are you crazy!" Porsche lunged at Tasty but stopped short when she pulled out a blade. "What bitch? You gonna cut me?" she asked.

"If I have to," she said and motioned towards the couch against the wall. "Now sit your ass down."

Porsche did as she was told. She sat down and looked up at Tasty, "So what the fuck is this about?" she asked.

"Bitch you knew!" Tasty screamed. "You been fucking Kane then got the nerve to waltz up in my home girl's club thinking you hot shit!"

Porsche started to go in on her. "What I'm doing or who I'm doing is none of your fucking business! Not yours or that bald, red bitch, Toya. I'll beat both-"

"You'll what?" said another voice.

Porsche turned to see Toya walking out of the shadows. *Where in the hell did this bitch come from?* she thought to herself, but instead she said, "So what? I'm supposed to be scared? Y'all bitches gonna jump me now?"

They remained silent.

They remained silent.

"If y'all jump me y'all better kill me because my bitches coming back for that ass!"

Suddenly, Tasty punched her in the mouth. The next thing she knew, she was taking punches from every direction and tasting blood.

"Arrrghhh!" she managed to scream as she felt the blade pierce her side. All she could do was call out for her sister and fold up into a fetal position. All she wanted to do was protect her baby. She grimaced in pain as she felt her arm being sliced open. She was hurting so bad and trying not to succumb to the pain, but she felt her body shut down against her will as she blacked out.

When she finally came to, she slowly opened her eyes. She shut them back quickly when she was met with the bright light hanging above her. She cautiously opened her eyes again and looked around to see her sister run to her side. Beside her where Charese and her friend Courtni. She started coughing and Charese ran to the other side of the bed to give her some water. She painfully took the water down. She looked at her girls, Mimi on one side, Charese on the other and a tear fell from her eye as they both held her hands. She tried to speak but Charese wouldn't let her.

She wouldn't listen. Her voice ached and was very raspy as she spoke, "Where's everybody else?" she whispered.

"Justin left to take a shower, but he's coming right back baby, nobody is leaving your side and Mommy is on her way," Mimi assured her little sister. She stroked her hair as she laid her forehead against Porsche's. Everyone in the room was in tears.

"And my baby?" Porsche questioned.

Buckets of tears fell from Mimi's face.

"There was nothing they could do," Mimi said as she held her head down.

Porsche started crying hysterically.

"I'm going to make them pay sister, I promise."

Porsche started crying harder and choking between sobs. Charese tried to calm her down but to no avail. She started coughing up blood. Mimi screamed and pushed Charese while Courtni ran out into the crowded hallway to get help.

"Call the fucking doctor Reesy! Lord, please don't take my sister!"

That was the last thing Porsche heard Mimi say as she felt her sister hug her tight. She wanted to hug her back so badly, but her body was too weak. She felt herself slipping away and wanted to do nothing but stay and comfort her sister.

The doctor rushed into the room but was too late, Porsche flat lined. Mimi started screaming uncontrollably and wouldn't let her go. Security and nurses had to escort her and Charese out of the room. The team did their best to revive her, but they were not successful. Porsche Shaw was pronounced dead.

Chapter Nine

ONE YEAR LATER

Charese stared at herself in the mirror. She was now a licensed cosmetologist, but she couldn't be happy like she wanted to. So much had happened in the last year. Her cousin Porsche was murdered a week before her birthday, and shortly after that her Uncle Charles passed away from a heart attack. She and her Aunt Kathy were okay because Uncle Charles had life insurance. Aunt Kathy had taken to alcohol and was drunk in her room ninety percent of the time. Poor Mimi took a turn for the worse after her sister passed. Their mother had to take care of her children because Mimi had no strength to take care of them herself and was dependent on antidepressants.

She had to move in with Mimi during the first three months after Porsche's passing because she was suicidal. Now, she was slowly beginning to be herself again.

Toya and Tasty's trial went by fast. They both received a sentence twenty years and were already serving their sentences. Porsche's death was a big shock to everyone, especially when it came out that she was pregnant by Kane. Kane didn't care about either of them and was still up to his same ways. Being true to his nature, he was still running thots in and out of his club and houses. Charese and Tee had been officially dating for about six months, but of course she was still having the best sex of her life with Tip, unbeknownst to everyone else. She ate Tip's pussy more than she sucked Tee's dick. She just couldn't get enough of her. She and Bryce had become really good friends; he had really been there for her. He acted like a real friend, but she could tell that he still liked her.

She fluffed her hair once more before turning away from the mirror and walking out of the bathroom. She grabbed her phone and car keys and headed out the door. She was about to go register for college. Since she now had her license, she was planning on going to school to pursue business management degree. She wanted to own her own salon one day. Until then, she was doing hair at home and making house calls. She refused to help fund someone else's dream. She decided to call and check on Mimi while en route to the campus.

"Hello," Mimi groggily answered on the fourth ring.

"Her cuz, how are you doing?" Charese asked.

"Hey, I'm getting the kids back today. Tonio is over here preparing for them now," Mimi replied.

"Are you getting them back for good?" Charese inquired.

"Yes, I miss them," Mimi confirmed.

"I know you do," Charese said. She felt so bad for Mimi because she and Porsche weren't only sisters, they were best friends.

"Justin came by today," Mimi stated.

"Oh really?" Charese said surprised.

"Yeah, he said he wanted to see how I was doing and say goodbye before he left for Cali. He got a job offer out there."

"Cali?" Charese asked.

"Yeah, he said he had nothing left here and he missed Porsche too much to stay around," she said but she started crying before she could even finish her sentence.

Charese tried to calm her down but she could tell that Mimi was still hurting. She heard a lot of noise and then Tonio's voice on the line.

"Who is this?" he asked.

"Reesy, why?" she countered. He surprised her by not coming back with a smart remark. It was no secret that they didn't care for each other.

She had been in the lobby of the school waiting on her paperwork while they were on the phone. The receptionist finally handed her a manila folder and she left the school.

"Look, I'm about to lay her down so she won't be so emotional when the kids get here. I'll have her call you back ok?"

"Yea, okay no problem," she said and disconnected the call and called Tee.

"Hey," he said when he answered.

"Hey, what you doing?" she asked.

"Shit, chillin with the boys."

"Oh ok."

"Why? What's up?" he asked, sounding like he was rushing her off the phone.

"What's up? Damn, I gotta have a reason to call you now?" she asked, aggravated.

"Nah," he paused, "I'm just kind of busy right now. Let me call you back."

He hung up on her before she could even protest.

Let me find out this nigga tryna play me already, she thought to herself. She was halfway home when her phone rang. It was Bryce. She answered as she stopped at a red light.

"Hello," she said.

"Where you going?" he asked.

"What?" asked a confused Charese.

"Look behind you."

She did and met a smiling Bryce. She couldn't help but smile.

"Are you following me?" she asked.

"Only if you don't mind," he said flirtatiously. Honestly, Charese thought he was actually cute. She would fuck him.

"Turn at the next light and park in the mall's parking lot," he ordered.

She agreed. He parked beside her as she was getting out of the car. She approached him as he was getting out of a Yukon that she knew wasn't his.

"Boy who car you done stole?" she asked as they embraced each other.

Damn he smells good, she thought to herself.

"I told you that you be sleeping on your boy B. You can have one too if you act right," he smiled.

"Yea right, what's up?" she questioned.

"Well, I know that your twenty-first birthday is next week. I know you didn't have much to celebrate last year and I'ma be out of town for your birthday this year. So I thought, hey, why not treat you early," he said.

"Is that right?" she countered.

"Yea, and besides, you probably gonna be with your girls or that punk ass nigga you've been kicking it with," he stated with a hint of jealousy in his voice.

"Let me find out you're jealous!" Charese smirked.

"Get in," he demanded with authority.

She got into the car not knowing their destination. They ended up going to eat at California Dreaming in Greenville and then went shopping at the Haywood Mall where Bryce dropped two stacks on her like it didn't even phase his pockets. Of course, she didn't complain. When they returned from Greenville, he dropped her off at her car. She grabbed her bags, gave him a kiss on the cheek, and thanked him for a lovely evening. She got into her car and they said goodbye.

Chapter Ten

"Damn nigga, Reesy gonna kick your ass if she find out you're stepping out on her man," Vic said.

"How she gonna know unless one of y'all motherfuckers tell her?" Tee questioned.

"Shit, you just better watch your back, you and her!" Vic said referring to the girl that Tee was laid up on the couch with. The girl didn't say a word.

"All I'm saying is this shit is deeper than you think. Shit gonna get real if Reesy finds out about it."

"Nigga, go ahead with that bullshit," Tee hollered.

"I'm just saying man, you fuckin' with this bitch of all people," Vic said, referring to the girl again.

"Who are you calling a bitch?" the girl asked, twisting her neck in his direction.

"Nigga, don't disrespect my girl," Tee said calmly.

"Yo girl? Nigga!" Vic started laughing so hard he became teary eyed. "You better be glad Charese won't fuck wit me because I would gladly take her off of your hands."

Tee looked at him menacingly but said nothing.

"Baby, don't worry about him or Charese," the girl said to Tee as she passionately kissed him.

"Hell, I'm not," he assured her. "Let's go to your spot."

They walked past Vic without saying a word as they left. They got into Tee's Maxima and rode in silence all the way to her house in Belton. Tee was thinking of Charese; he loved her, but she had so much going on. This girl was just another bitch to him, something to do. He didn't love her nor did he care about her. Unbeknownst to Tee, she was also thinking of Charese. She couldn't stand her and she felt the same way about Tee that he felt about her. Tee was just her payback; Charese Shaw wasn't shit to her. She would spit on that bitch if she could.

She couldn't understand why all of the niggas in the city went crazy over her. She was just another undercover thot like the rest of her home girls. Tee was lost in his own thoughts and not paying her any attention. She looked at herself in her compact mirror, moved a piece of hair from her eyes, and reapplied her lipstick. She knew she was fine, regardless of bitches like Charese standing in her way thinking they were God's gift to a nigga. She was 5'10, but well proportioned. She resembled supermodel Tyra Banks. Personally, she thought she looked better than Charese.

His phone rang and began to yell into the phone. She knew it was Charese. He ended the call and threw it down in his lap.

"Damn," was all he said.

"Don't worry boo, I'm about to take good care of you," she said as she rubbed his dick through his pants.

He smiled, but his mind was elsewhere.

Chapter Eleven

"I'm so sick and tired of him," Charese cried out in frustration after she hung up on Tee. She went through her phone until she came across Courtni's number and called her best friend.

"What's up girl?" Courtni asked when she answered.

"Shit, just got off the phone arguing with Tee's dumb ass." She blew an exasperated breath into the phone.

"Again?" Courtni exclaimed.

"Yes, and I'm ready to pull my hair out," Charese screamed.

"Girl, don't even give him the satisfaction," Courtni said.

"You're right, how does going out tonight sound?" Charese inquired.

"I'm cool wit it," Courtni said in agreement.

"Cool, well, I'ma call everybody and we can meet up at Tip's house," Charese stated.

"Bet," Courtni said.

They ended their call and Charese called her girls and let them know about the plans she made for the night, then went home to get ready.

After showering, she pinned her hair up into a high bun then started getting dressed. She chose a hot pink Polo dress with some green and pink heels to wear for the night. She sprayed on a little perfume and then headed for Tip's house. She was first to arrive, then Courtni and Taye.

Taye was one of her close friends too but she didn't hang out much because she worked twelve hour shifts, raised two twin boys alone, and went to school part time.

"I know that ain't Tasia Johnson rising from the dead?" Charese teased as Taye walked through the door.

"Hey y'all," Taye said as she hugged each of her girls then took a seat at the kitchen table. She poured herself a shot of the Patron that was sitting in the middle of the table. Taye was a big girl, but she carried herself well and she was beautiful inside and out. She had no problem getting a man just like the rest of her friends. She was Raven Symone's complexion, 5'9, probably between 200 and 220 pounds, her hair was in a short hairstyle similar to Anita Baker's, and dressed well. She was doing her thing. A boss bitch in her own right.

"So what you been up to girl?" Tip was asking Taye.

"Shit girl, raising them boys of mine, ready to bust that baby daddy up!" she said and they all laughed.

They chilled while Tip showered and dressed then they left for the club. Tip looked amazing in a tight, form fitting yellow dress that barely covered her ass and some white heels. Charese had to admit that Tip looked damn good and she wanted some of that juicy pussy right then and there, but she ignored her urges as she helped Courtni adjust her halter-top. Courtni was wearing a red halter with a black belt around her waist, black booty shorts, and red heels. Taye was wearing a blue, black and brown vest over a form fitting white tee, black low-rise jeans, and brown suede thigh high boots.

They headed to a bar in Belton. The Belton Bar was a little spot they hit up on occasion. Once they arrived they ordered two pitchers of Vodka and went to find a table.

Paparazzi tryna take pictures tell them folks get the fuck out my face. I don't fuck wit twelve cuz I heard they been listening to a nigga conversation -

"Oh shit, that's my song!" Taye said as she grabbed her drink and headed towards the dance floor. Charese was watching her girl dance by herself when a fine ass man approached her. They danced for a while then went to the bar. Following suit, Charese headed to the bar for a refill.

"What can I get you sexy?" the female bartender asked Charese, obviously flirting.

"Let me get a shot of E&J," Charese requested and handed her a ten-dollar bill.

She didn't take it. "Nah, that dude over there said he got it," she said while simultaneously pointing to her left.

Charese looked in that direction until her eyes fell on Trap and he had the audacity to be headed in her direction!

"Nah," she said as she pressed the ten-dollar bill into the bartender's hand. "I can buy my own damn drinks."

"Damn, why you keep acting like that Reesy?" Trap said as he approached her.

"Nigga, do you really want to go there?" she threatened. "I've already put your business on my page don't make me tell the club!"

"Man, go 'head with that bullshit!" he warned.

She turned to walk away but he forcefully grabbed her arm and she jerked it away from him.

"Don't be grabbing on me like that motherfucker!" she yelled.

"Hold up bitch!" he said as he jacked her up. "You acting like you wasn't just sucking my dick before you started suckin' on that new nigga. Bitch you ain't grand! You think those damn screenshots are funny?" he started choking her.

She dropped the glass that was in her hand and started swinging wildly. She looked and saw security headed their way, but Courtni beat them to her. Out of nowhere, Courtni hit Trap between the eyes with a bottle. Then Taye came from behind and kicked him in the nuts. He dropped Charese on the floor and chaos erupted all around them. Courtni was yelling for Tip as security began pushing them out the door. Just then, a different fight broke out. Security dropped the girls and went to handle the fight that had started between three men. They all headed to Courtni's car, she unlocked the doors and they climbed in. Charese let her window down so that she could get some fresh air and regain her composure. Just then she felt someone grab her hair and try to pull her through the window.

"You raggedy bitch! You think you cute?" Trap said with his face covered in blood and a look in his eyes that scared Charese. He started punching her square in the face like she was a man. Taye got out the car and pulled out her gun.

"Don't make me shoot that infected dick off nigga," Taye said with much seriousness in her tone.

He looked at her like she was crazy as she took the safety off. He let go of Charese and backed up with his hands in the air. Taye helped her into the car and Courtni sped off. Tip was trying to attend to Charese who was slipping in and out of consciousness. She had blood leaking from her nose, mouth, and right ear. They hauled ass to the nearest store that was open and parked in the parking lot. Tip was holding Charese while Taye got out and ran into the store.

Charese couldn't believe this shit; that nigga really just tried to kill her. She looked at Courtni who had a panicked expression on her face. Just then, Taye came running out of the store with someone behind her. Charese tried to make out who it was, but before they even got close enough for her to see their face, she blacked out. Her world was dark.

Chapter Twelve

"I know one of y'all niggas got a cigar?" Seven asked his boys.

"Nah, let's go to the store," Bryce said.

They were all chillin at Kat's house. The store was right up the street. Bryce grabbed his car keys and walked out the door with Seven right behind him. Seven was a big nigga; he got his name from his height. He was seven feet even, 300 pounds, and had hands that were the size of a grapefruit when he balled his fist up. He and Bryce became friends a while back when some shit went down and he saved Bryce's life. They didn't even know each other, but Seven felt that it was his duty to get involved. They'd been as thick as thieves ever since.

They arrived at the store and went in to get what they needed. Bryce stood in line for the cigars and Seven went to the back to grab a case of beer. Bryce was telling Seven to grab a Red Bull for him when a girl came running into the store crying and begging for help. The clerk came from behind the counter and she started tugging on the oversized white man's clothes trying to get him to follow her but he was clearly frightened. That's when she laid eyes on Bryce.

She ran to him. "Please, you have to help her," she insisted.

Bryce looked at the girl; she looked very familiar to him, but he couldn't place her face. Bryce followed her outside with the store clerk right behind them. He immediately recognized Courtni in the driver's seat. She was turned around looking in the back with a look of terror on her face. It was then that Bryce noticed Charese stretched out in the back seat covered in blood and he began to panic. He took off running towards the car.

"Reesy, wake up!" said a crying Taye who was trying to smack her friend awake.

He opened the door and told Taye to move. He checked to see if she was still breathing and thank God she was.

"Why didn't y'all take her to a fucking hospital?" Bryce demanded answers.

"I panicked," Courtni said in between sobs.

"What the fuck happened?" he asked.

Tip told him about the episode they just had with Trap at the club. The store clerk handed Bryce a cold rag.

"Would you like me to call an ambulance?" asked the nervous man.

"Nah, I got her. Thanks for your help my mans," Bryce said and nodded at Seven who was standing beside Taye trying to comfort her. Seven reached into his pocket and pulled out a one hundred dollar bill. He handed it to the clerk and he graciously accepted it. He turned and walked into the store before they changed their minds and wanted the money back.

"I'm gonna take her with me, she's good," Bryce told them.

None of the girls tried to protest.

*****

Charese started stirring in her sleep, which immediately got Bryce's undivided attention. They were alone and she had been asleep for the past twenty-four hours, but Bryce felt it was best to leave her be. His boys had their ears to the street around the clock. They were all looking for Trap who seemed to have gone into hiding. Bryce had already put a price on his head. Nobody was gonna hurt Charese and get away with it if he could help it. His phone had been going off all day. He was missing money, but he had to ensure Charese's safe keeping. Her phone was constantly going off as well. It amazed him and pissed him off how she had all of these missed calls from everyone but the nigga she was fucking with. He went to fix her a glass of water and then returned to her side. He admired her beauty as he watched her sleep. She slowly opened her eyes and looked around. Unaware of her surroundings, she began to panic. Then she laid eyes on Bryce and her look went from one of pure terror to relief and concern.

She cleared her throat. "Where my girls at?" she asked.

"I sent them away, I got you ma," Bryce said with confidence.

Charese grabbed her phone and rolled her eyes after looking through it. She threw it back on the bed.

"I can't believe this nigga," she mumbled under her breath.

Bryce grabbed her by the face and kissed her passionately, using his tongue to circle her full, pouty lips. He broke the kiss and she stared at him in disbelief. He had rendered her speechless.

"You ain't gotta worry about shit lil' mama, I got you, that's my word!" Bryce said reassuringly.

Chapter Thirteen

Charese had been at Bryce's house for almost two weeks while she healed. No one knew where she was but her girls. She wasn't answering her phone for Tee for two reasons. One, he waited three days after the accident to call her and, two, she had had sex with Bryce three times since she had been there and she now had mixed emotions. She was alone on the couch flipping through the TV channels. Bryce went out to get her a cheeseburger plate and a sweet tea; she was getting hungrier by the minute just thinking about the food. She hoped that he didn't forget her brown gravy for her fries. She had to have her brown gravy.

She was still flipping through the channels on the 52-inch and stopped on the ten o'clock news when she saw Trap's face on the screen. Apparently, his dismembered body was found in a dumpster earlier that morning. She covered her mouth in shock and gasped just as Bryce was walking through the door with their food. He hung up his phone as he set the food down on the coffee table.

"You good Reesy?" he asked.

"Yea, hand me my food," she said.

They ate in silence. She knew that he had to be behind Trap's murder, but she spoke nothing of it.

Later that night, Bryce dropped her off at home. He gave her a little change to help her get herself together. She was unsure of what to do but by the time Bryce dropped her off, she had her mind made up; she was leaving Tee. She had real feelings for him, but Bryce handled her with so much care and deep down her heart yearned for that type of affection. They had a long talk while she stayed with him. He wanted to take care of her and help her get on her feet. She was gonna let him spoil her if he wanted to. She took a shower and changed into a sweat suit then straightened her hair, letting it hang loose. She decided to call and check on Mimi on her way back out the door.

Mimi answered. "Damn bitch I'm glad you finally decided to let somebody know you were okay. Don't do that again," she scolded

"And how have you been?" Charese asked her, completely dismissing everything she had just said.

"I'm good and so are the kids, but I should be asking you that," she said sincerely.

"I'm alright, I'm about to go fill out some apartment applications and finish enrolling in Tech," Charese informed her.

"Oh that's good Reesy!" Mimi exclaimed.

"Yep, I'm about to get a degree in business management in hopes of opening my own salon one day," she proudly stated.

"Well that's good. Me and Tonio are doin' really good. I had to get in your girl Donikka's shit because she claimed they were still fucking," she said with a hint of jealousy in her voice.

"And they probably are," Charese said flatly.

"Whatever Reesy, I got three of his kids," she stated matter-of-factly.

"And so does Megan," Charese reminded her.

"Damn Reesy, whose side are you on?" Mimi snapped.

"All I'm saying is when you're dealing with a bullshit nigga you accept the bullshit that he comes with. That's a typical thug nigga's behavior cuz," Charese said.

The line grew silent and Charese could sense the tension between them even through the phone. She tried to lighten the mood.

"Anyway, why don't I come over after I leave the school?" she asked

"I'll let you know. You know I got a lot of bullshit goin' on," she said, her voice laced with sarcasm.

Before Charese could say anything, Mimi hung up on her. *Oh well!* She thought. Her mind shifted to Bryce. She was really confused when it came to him. He was sweet, attentive, and the sex was amazing. Her ringing cell phone interrupted her thoughts. It was a private call, which she ignored; she didn't answer private calls. They called right back.

"Hello?" she answered but heard nothing. She looked at the phone, "Hello!"

All she heard was one word before they hung up the phone.

"Bitch!"

Chapter Fourteen

"Oh my gosh!" Shi Shi sighed loudly, "Will you answer that damn phone already!" she grabbed the phone from her nightstand and handed it to him. He grabbed it and flipped it over without looking at the caller ID.

"Who the fuck is this?" he barked into the phone.

"Yo, calm down nigga. I was just trying to check on your girl, Tee, damn!" He recognized the voice as Vic's. *What?* He thought as he sat up in bed.

"Man, what the hell you talking about?" he demanded.

"So you don't know? You haven't talked to her, hold up, where you at bruh?" asked an inquisitive Vic.

"That's not important."

Vic cut him off, "Well, what is important is the shit that's goin' down with your old lady. Trap beat your bitch's ass and you over there laid up in that nasty pussy."

"Nasty pussy? Who the fuck is Trap?" he demanded answers.

Shi Shi's eyes bulged out of her head and she sat up. Five minutes later, she watched Tee put on his clothes and rush out of the house without even saying goodbye.

He raced back to Anderson trying desperately to reach Charese, but she wouldn't answer so he called Vic back.

"So this Trap nigga mad because my bitch don't want him and laid hands on her?" Tee screamed into the phone when Vic answered.

"He's her ex," Vic answered nonchalantly.

Tee got angry all over again. "So they're beefin' because she doesn't want him anymore more?"

"I guess that's part of it," Vic said.

"What you mean? Don't talk in circles nigga," Tee said.

"My guess is that nasty bitch you fuckin' with. She the main reason they beefin," Vic informed.

"Who? Shi Shi?" Tee asked.

"Yea nigga, look, I gotta take my girl to work. I'll get with you later," Vic said and hung up the phone.

Damn, I fucked up he thought to himself while wondering how Reesy and Shi Shi knew each other. He tried to call Charese again.

****

Three days had passed and he still wasn't able to reach Charese. Shi Shi had been calling, but he ignored every call. He wanted to know how she connected the dots, but he wanted to hear Charese's side of the story first. He had heard about Trap's death and he had also heard it was because of what he did to Charese. He could understand her being mad because he called so late after it happened, but that didn't mean she had to keep ignoring him the way he had. It made him wonder who she was with and what she was doing, which was probably just his own guilt.

He was at Ingles doing some grocery shopping when he noticed Taye with her kids. He didn't know her that well, but he knew that she was Charese's friend. He approached her as she was chastising one child and fixing the hair of another.

"Yo, where Reesy at?" he commanded.

"Well, hello to you too. She's fine," Taye flatly stated.

"Okay, but where she at?" Tee reiterated.

"I can't disclose that information," she said.

He got so close to her that she could smell the mouthwash on his breath. He didn't give a fuck about her kids being there, but what he didn't know was neither did she.

She opened her purse so he could see her .380. "Nigga, I don't give a fuck about being in Ingles." She stepped even closer. "If you ever in your life try to step to me like that again I will drop you where you stand."

73

She looked him dead in the eyes. They stared at each other for a minute, neither breaking their stare until Taye felt one of her boys tug at her shirt. She shook her head and walked past him, slightly bumping into him.

"Come on boys," she said without even looking back.

Tee stood there in disbelief for a second and then continued on with his grocery shopping.

After he finished grocery shopping, he put his groceries in the trunk and sat in the car. He thought about Charese then thought about Shi Shi. He still didn't know what the beef between them was, but Charese was acting like a bitch right now and Shi Shi was always ready. Ready for him to call and say he was on his way to come fuck her. He loved pussy, and right now he needed some.

He called Shi Shi. She picked up on the first ring and he told her that he was on the way over.

"Have that pussy ready," he said and hung up the phone. He left Ingles and headed to Belton.

Chapter Fifteen

Courtni had just gotten back from Tony's house. She had finally forgiven him for cheating and he assured her that it wouldn't happen again. She promised herself that if he cheated one more time, it was the end of the road for them. She was sick of these random bitches popping up out of nowhere. A few had even claimed to have been pregnant by her man. He was her man, so why was she sharing him with every thot in Anderson County? It was late and she was looking forward to a bubble bath and a blunt. She lived with her mom and sister's, but they all had third shift jobs so she was looking forward to the alone time. It was two in the morning and she was tired as hell.

She pulled out her keys and had the house key ready for entry as soon as she opened her car door. It was out of habit even though she knew everybody in Mount Vernon; the apartment complex she lived in. Besides, no one was out at this hour except the local drug dealers and she had already slept with the majority of them in high school. She had no worries, but she couldn't shake the eerie feeling that was hovering over her. She grabbed her pocketbook and locked the car door as she stepped out of the car. She had no idea why she was paranoid, but something just didn't seem right. Her cell phone rang, startling her, and she dropped her keys.

She sighed heavily and ignored the call, which was from Tony. She picked up her keys and just as she did, she felt someone grab her from behind. She started screaming but the large hands covering her mouth muffled her cries. She did the first thing that came naturally to her; she began kicking and bit the hand. Because they were wearing leather gloves, her attempts were futile. She kicked, and clawed until she felt her head being slammed into a hard object, and she blacked out.

****

Charese plopped down on the couch, glad to be home. She had just gotten back from Seneca. She, Mimi, and her kids went to spend the weekend with their grandmother. They both had wanted to get out of Anderson. It was Sunday night and she wanted to go out to relieve some of the stress that she was under. Someone had been playing on her phone since Thursday, in reference to what, she was still in the dark, but she was agitated and equally nervous.

She was beside herself as to what to do. She talked to Taye over the weekend, but had not heard from Courtni or Tip. She tried to reach Courtni on numerous occasions. Just then, her phone rang. She looked at it and saw 'Unknown Number' flash across the screen so she ignored it and they called right back. Charese answered with a very nasty attitude.

"What the fuck do you want u scared little pussy?" she barked into the phone.

"Not your washed up ass, bitch," was the reply.

They hung up the phone. She couldn't help but wonder who it was and what they wanted. She was about to call Bryce when her phone rang again. This time it was Courtni.

She answered and said, "Girl where the hell you been? Somebody's been playing on my phone tearing my nerves up!" she awaited a response but all she heard was a lot of crying and moaning.

"Courtni?" Charese paused, "Courtni!"

"She's going to die bitch. Your next," said a man's voice.

Charese froze; she recognized the man's voice as the same one that had called her a bitch before. This time they were calling from her best friend's phone and she

77

immediately began to panic. What in the hell was going on? Just as she was about to speak she heard Courtni moan and begged them to stop. Charese began to cry.

"This for my nigga Trap," the voice said.

"You leave her alone you bastard!" Charese screamed into the phone.

"This bitch is going to die and it's a shame because that pussy sweet too," said the voice. They hung up before she could protest anymore. Hysterical with tears streaming down her face, she tried to call back over and over again, but they would never answer. She called Bryce.

"What's up mama?" he asked when he answered.

Charese couldn't talk. She tried to stop crying.

"Yo, calm down ma. What's wrong? You have to stop crying and talk to me.

Still, she cried.

"I can't fix it if you don't talk to me Charese."

She softened her cries to sniffles and told Bryce what had just happened.

"What the fuck?" he screamed into the phone.

"They took her!" Charese began to cry again.

"Look ma, relax, I need you to meet me at my lil spot in Belton. I'ma handle these niggas. Stringer Street, do you know where Stringer Street is?" he asked.

"Yes," Charese whispered. She could hear his boys in the background screaming they were ready for war and down for whatever.

"Calm down, Reesy. I promise I got you. Just come to Belton like I told you," he assured her.

She agreed and they hung up the phone. She went into her aunt's closet and got her .22 out of her shoebox. It all made sense now, all this bullshit fell back on Trap's ass. He was fuckin with her! She didn't have him killed, Bryce did that shit on his own and now her best friend was paying for it. This was all Bryce's fault so he was going to help her get Courtni back before they killed her. They were already raping her and just that thought alone made Charese nauseous. She didn't even want to imagine what else they were doing to her. They were torturing Courtni in hopes of getting to her so now she had two additional problems on top of the ones that the already had. That's where Bryce and those thugs he ran with came in. But just who were these people and what did they want from her? If they were willing to abduct Courtni, how far would they go? And would they come for her next? Just those thoughts alone overwhelmed her and she burst into tears.

She couldn't stop crying as she drove to Belton. She kept checking her rearview mirror, afraid that someone was following her. They had to be watching her if they were watching Courtni. How else would they have taken her? Or knew when to take her? She turned off Smythe Street and onto Stringer Street. As soon as she turned onto the street, she noticed Bryce in one yard with his friends arguing with someone. She parked and got out of the car and noticed that that someone was Tee.

Chapter Sixteen

Tee lay in bed eating the spaghetti that Shi Shi had just put together. After the fuck session they just had, he had worked up an appetite. She was in the shower and he was still butt naked under her covers. His phone rang; he didn't want to talk to the caller so he ignored the call. He noticed that his phone was dying so he slipped on his pants so that he could go retrieve his cell phone's charger from his car. "Yo, my man's let me holla at you," he heard someone say. He knew no one in the area so he kept walking.

"Aye bruh, you fuck wit Reesy right?" he heard the voice say.

That stopped him in the tracks and he turned to see who was talking to him. He didn't recognize the man standing before him.

He said, "What's up man?" with a lot of attitude.

"Yea, that's that nigga," said the large man standing beside him.

"You got beef nigga?" Tee asked the man.

"Hell yea nigga!" the man said as he stepped forward. "I'm out here taking care of your bitch while you over there fuckin Shi Shi of all people. And I want your bitch! Hell yea I got a problem! I don't like you bruh!"

"Bryce chill," the large man said as he grabbed his shoulder and pointed in the direction of the car that had just parked in the yard.

Charese got out of the car looking in both directions. *What in the hell was going on? Does Tee know about me and Bryce? What in the hell is he doing here anyway? Whose house is that?* All these thoughts ran through Charese's mind as she looked at the two men in her life. She walked to the front of her car. She looked from Tee to Bryce, both looking equally angry. She looked at Bryce once again, but it was Tee whom she addressed first.

"What are you doing here?" she asked him.

He didn't answer her, instead her just stared at her. She walked across the street to where he was standing.

"Tee what's going on?" she asked full of concern.

He ignored her and turned his attention to B-man.

"Damn you little snitch nigga. You called my bitch out here?" he asked raising his voice.

Charese looked at Bryce. "What the fuck is going on?" she repeated herself.

"Man, don't even worry about that bitch ass nigga Reesy, I told you I got you anyway! You got too much goin' on to be worried about him," Bryce said.

Tee snapped, "Nigga fuck you! I'll whoop all y'all asses!" he yelled getting big in the chest.

That got the whole crowd rowdy. Nosey neighbors were coming out of their houses, standing on their porches, and some were even walking closer towards the action to get a better view of the drama that was unfolding.

"What the fuck is going on out here?" they heard a female's voice say. Charese looked towards the house and there stood Shi Shi in nothing but a towel. She was standing in the yard that Tee's car was parked in. Shi Shi was on the porch with a freaking towel on, and Tee didn't have a shirt on.

"What the fuck? Hold the fuck up!" Charese said getting angrier by the minute.

She hit Tee in his chest. "What the fuck is this shit?"

He looked cold busted and the surprised look on his face confirmed everything that she already knew. That bitch got her again. That was an ass whooping in her book.

She mushed Tee in the head with her index finger. "You fucking this bitch too?"

He looked confused, but didn't say anything.

"You fucking this bitch?" she asked a little louder pointing at Shi Shi and looking menacingly at her.

This time Charese addressed her. "Bitch, you didn't get enough from the last ass whooping?" she yelled.

Shi Shi stood there frozen in place, the fear evident on her face.

Tee reached for Charese. "Reesy," he said.

She jerked away from him and started walking towards the house. The spectators all grew loud with excitement and anticipation ready for the fight they were sure was about to happen. There was a combination of "uh-oh's" and "whoa's" as Charese walked up the stairs. A few brave souls were even in the yard with their phones already on record. It was then that Tee tried to run after Charese.

"Bitch you better not step foot-" that was all Shi Shi managed to get out of her mouth before Charese hit her with a haymaker that sent her flying back into the house.

As Tee was walking up the stairs, Charese was shutting Shi Shi's front door. She heard people saying "Oh shit" as she locked it behind her.

Shi Shi got up holding her face, but before she could even move, Charese pounced on her.

"Bitch I told you that I would fucking kill you if you ever crossed me again!" she warned as she punched her repeatedly. All Shi Shi could do was try and guard her face. They heard Tee banging on the door demanding that Charese open it, but Charese was not leaving until she gave Shi Shi the ass whooping of her life. She kicked her in her stomach repeatedly, making her remove her hands from her face to guard her stomach.

As soon as Shi Shi exposed her face, Charese kicked her in the nose causing blood to spill out onto the carpet. Charese grabbed her by the hair and beat her head against the coffee table. Poor Shi Shi could do nothing but beg for mercy causing Charese to laugh as she hit her with a mean right hook. Charese heard Tee trying to break the door down but she was still whooping Shi Shi's ass. Shi Shi's head met Charese's fist a few more times before she started crying uncontrollably and just gave up her worthless attempts to protect herself.

She was bleeding from her nose and mouth before Charese finally stopped. Out of breath, Charese stood up and looked down at Shi Shi. She shook her head before she walked over to her and walked into the kitchen. She took a soda from the refrigerator and drank most of it down in one gulp.

Shi Shi had managed to sit up, but was still crying. She wouldn't look at Charese, but she said, "Get out of my house before I call the police!"

Charese walked over to her and poured the remaining soda over her head then walked over to the door and unlocked it.

Chapter Seventeen

Bryce watched as Tee attempted to break down the door. *Look at this fool* he thought to himself. What he couldn't believe was that Charese was brave enough to walk into that girl's house like that. He thought it was sexy as hell and it made him want her even more.

"Damn, shorty got a lot of heart," Kat said.

They all winced as they heard glass breaking. A few laughed when they heard Shi Shi begging her to stop.

"Let me go get my lil' mama," Bryce said with a smirk on his face.

He started to walk across the street but as soon as he reached the yard, Charese opened the door.

"WorldStar!" a lot of people screamed with their cell phones in hand. A couple of people were standing at the door recording Shi Shi.

"Charese," Tee said as he reached for her.

She jerked away and walked right past him like he wasn't even there. She met Bryce in the yard and he put his arm around her as they walked back across the street. He looked over his shoulder and winked at Tee who just stood there dumbfounded.

*****

The big burly man's thrust disgusted Courtni. The sweat that was pouring from his body and into her eyes disgusted her even more. He grunted loudly as he pulled out and released himself on her face. She thought she was about to vomit as she sniffled quietly. She learned to stop screaming a long time ago after being beaten every time she did. She was sticky, her vagina was very sore, and she smelled terrible. She was emotionally exhausted and she wanted to die. If them killing her was the only way to escape the hell that she was in then she welcomed it now rather than later.

He got up and another man flopped down on the soiled mattress that she was lying on. He pulled out his manhood and rubbed it along her face. She cringed at his touch as he fondled her breast. Her nipples were hard, not from pleasure, but from the cold air that they had circulating in the dark basement. She was as naked as the day she was born. She was stuck in the basement with three men who had all violated her repeatedly. They took turns on her, they made her perform oral on them, and she had been fucked in both holes more times than she cared to remember. She couldn't see who they were because they kept their entire faces covered except their eyes.

"Let's call that bitch back," the man said to Courtni as he pushed her head into his groin causing her to choke on the penis that was in her throat. She listened intensely as the man talked to someone on the phone.

"Who the fuck is this? Oh yea? Nigga fuck you! Put that bitch Charese on the phone! Nah nigga, I run the show! Well if you wanna see this bitch alive then you'll meet me tonight at two am sharp with fifty g's. I'll send you the location." He hung up the phone and handed it to his man's before grabbing Courtni by the hair and slinging her on the ground. He flipped her over on her stomach and roughly entered her from behind.

"Bitch your pussy stank, but it's still good though!" he said in between grunts.

"Fuck you!" she yelled through fresh tears.

He began to thrust harder until he finally reached his climax. He made her turn around and open her mouth as he ejaculated on her tongue.

"Swallow it bitch," he said through clenched teeth.

She spit it out. He grabbed the nearest gun and hit her over the head with it. Courtni took an involuntary nap once again.

When she finally woke up, she was in a car. They had just taken a turn on a dirt road behind a vacant building.

She had no clue where she was or what time it was. Through her good eye, she noticed that her assailants had picked up an extra man who was in the passenger's seat. All she could see was the back of his head so she did not know who he was. She looked down at herself and noticed she was still naked and began to cry.

She hated Charese right now; she had nothing to do with this bullshit. If Charese didn't save her, she would never forgive her. She held her breath as they came to a complete stop. Everyone got out of the car except her and the man in the passenger's seat. He turned to look at her and smiled a sinister smile. Her eyes were wide with fear when she saw his face. He reached back and pinched one of her nipples then hands found their way to the opening between her legs. Just one little finger caused her unbearable pain because she was so raw. But still, she let him molest her simply because of who he was. She was afraid of him just like everybody else.

Chapter Eighteen

"You ain't gotta worry about that nigga ma. I told you I will take care of you," Bryce told Charese.

"Let's just go in the house," Charese said trying to fight back tears. She heard someone comment on how much heart she had as she allowed Bryce to put his arms around her and lead her into the house. Tee was still standing in Shi Shi's yard looking dumbfounded. Just then, her cell phone rang. It was private so she handed it to Bryce; she knew it was them.

He answered with an attitude, "Whaddup bruh?" he asked. "Don't worry about who I am, but I know you got somebody that belong to me. Yea nigga, I bodied Trap! Nah nigga! Aight bet, I'll be there. Don't try no bullshit or I'm wettin' all your homies up!" He hung up the phone.

Charese was a nervous wreck. He looked at her and grabbed her by the face.

"It's gonna be aight mama, me and my niggas gonna ride with you to get your girl back, okay?"

She looked a little relieved. "Did they say what they wanted?" she asked.

Bryce told her about the fifty stacks that they demanded.

Charese became irate. "A ransom? A fucking ransom? Well you have to help me because if you wouldn't have killed Trap, they wouldn't be raping my best friend," she began to cry again.

He grabbed her and kissed her on the forehead. "Don't worry ma, we got you."

Charese stayed with Bryce and his boys for the remainder of the day. He had gotten her some KFC and she had access to Netflix and Hulu, so she stayed in bed in the back room while the men prepared for the warehouse meeting. Bryce told her that there was no way that he was giving up fifty thousand dollars, but he had a plan. He promised her that Courtni would be riding back with them.

It was 1:30 am when they reached their destination. Charese was on pins and needles. Unbeknownst to Charese, Bryce had some of his associates strategically placed around the area just in case shit went bad. He had people in the bushes, across the street, and behind the warehouse itself. They were parked in the grass and were the only car in sight. He had to call in a favor and got his boy Quint from Easley and his goons to watch his back because he didn't know these men or what they were capable of. They waited silently, everyone in their own thoughts.

Charese was hoping and praying that Courtni was returned to her safely. Bryce's adrenaline rush was at an all-time high and he was ready to drop every last one of them niggas where they stood. Seven was ready for whatever if Bryce was. Kat was growing tired of the thug life and decided then and there in the back seat that he was done. And Dub was hoping that he didn't get killed behind Charese and her bullshit. Wasn't no pussy worth all this trouble if you asked him. By 1:50 two cars pulled up and stopped directly in front of them. Charese recognized one of the cars, but couldn't remember where she saw it at. Bryce turned his headlights on and got out of the car but told Charese to stay inside.

"Nah fuck that, that's my best friend and it's my fault that she's in this mess," she said while getting out of the car.

Dub just shook his head thinking of how hard headed Charese was. Shit like that could get a nigga murked.

"Stay close to me," Bryce ordered.

She grabbed his hand. Two niggas with hoodies and sunglasses on got out of a Dodge Intrepid and stood before them. Another man got out of the Infiniti and gave

Bryce the 'what's up nigga' nod. He opened the passenger's door and a man got out of the car. Charese and Bryce both became angry with just the sight of him.

"What's up Charese?" he asked.

Chapter Nineteen

Charese watched as all the men got out of the car. She was still trying to remember where she had seen that Infiniti. One of the men opened the door to the Infiniti and a man stepped out and joined the other men.

"What's up Charese?" the man asked.

"Kane!" Charese said clearly in shock. She let go of Bryce's hand and charged at Kane, but he grabbed her by the waist.

"Chill Reesy," he said. Dub just shook his head.

"Whoa, be easy shawty," Kane said and snapped his fingers.

The same man went back to the Infiniti and this time Courtni emerged. Charese gasped when she saw the condition her friend was in and began to cry again. She tried to run to her, but Bryce had a death grip on her waist. They had fucked her friend up and now she was livid! Her lips were swollen and cracked, the left side of her face was bruised and purple, her left eye was swollen and had dried up blood around it. And not only did it look like dried up sperm on her hair and lips, but they had the nerve to have her out there butt naked and it was the end of October.

"Where my money at lil' nigga?" Kane asked Bryce.

95

"Give me Courtni then you'll get your money bitch," Bryce trying to keep his composure. He was growing angrier by the minute.

Kane looked at him like he was debating on something.

Charese wasn't any good to anybody right now. She watched as Kat retrieved a suitcase from the trunk of the car. She assumed it had the money in it, but she remembered Bryce saying that he wasn't giving him any money so she knew some shit was about to pop off.

"Get in the car," Bryce said to Charese.

She obeyed, but never took her eyes off Kane. If looks could kill then he would have been dead on the spot.

"Tell your mans to bring me Courtni then you can have your money," he said to Kane.

"What? Nigga, I call all the shots!" Kane yelled.

Bryce remained calm. "Not if you want this money you don't. My ole' lady wants her best friend back. Give her to me," he demanded.

Kat opened the suitcase and showed Kane the money. Kane looked at him sideways and chuckled then looked at the money and his eyes grew wild with excitement. He told his man to follow the orders; he had his hand on his gun just in case. He didn't know Bryce, and he looked like a pretty boy, but Kane knew he had a problem with him so he wasn't about to underestimate him. He was probably just another hatin' broke nigga like the rest of the men in Anderson. Kane knew he was that nigga and he knew it pissed everybody off.

Bryce never took his eyes off Kane as his man brought Courtni over to him. It pissed him off to look at her. He wanted to kill all of them right then and there, but thought better of it. Not with Charese and Courtni there. He had his hands on both his guns just in case Kane or one of his men tried anything stupid. The dude threw Courtni on the ground beside Bryce. She weakly stood up.

"Stand by me," Bryce said.

She grabbed his hand tight and was afraid to let go. She feared that if she let go she would discover that it was all a dream and she was still stuck in that basement. Seven grabbed her and put her in the car. The man returned to Kane with the suitcase in hand and Kane smiled. Bryce turned to get in the car.

"See you around," Kane said.

"You can bet your life on that nigga. Are we done here?" Bryce asked.

Kane looked at Kat then he nodded. "Yeah," he said as they got in the car.

Bryce got in his own car and took off his jacket handing it to Charese. She covered Courtni up with their jackets and they drove away. Kane wanted to shoot their car up but he knew better. He had peeped those niggas in the bushes and there was no telling how many more were out there lurking. They were outnumbered, but he knew that he would see that nigga again.

*****

"Yo nigga, I appreciate you watching my back man," Bryce said into his phone. He was thanking Quint.

Quint told him that it was nothing. He and Quint had been cool for a long time. Bryce used to jugg in Easley and found Quint in the trap. The trap was in a neighborhood they called "Across the hill". If you were from Easley then you knew that across the hill was drug central. They talked for a few more seconds then ended the call. He looked in the rearview mirror and watched as Charese consoled Courtni. He heard her apologize more than once. He felt bad for the both of them. On the outside, he seemed calm, cool, and collected, but on the inside, he was boiling.

He kept running into Kane making him want to kill him even more. He hated Kane with his whole being and he told himself that he would never forgive himself if he died before he took Kane's life. He rode the rest of the way in silence. All he kept thinking about was that fateful night.

"Yo, Unc! Ain't it about time for you to close up?" Bryce asked.

He helped his Uncle Jerry out from time to time. Jerry ran a liquor house and gambling spot out of his garage. It was renovated nicely. The liquor house was on the floor and the gambling rooms were upstairs. His Aunt Lori and their daughter, his cousin, Carmesha made the food, which was always blazing. They had the best wings in the entire Upstate.

"Yea, have Lori lock up, I had no idea it was after two," Uncle Jerry yelled from his office in the back.

Bryce walked to the counter and told his aunt to lock up while he resumed his cleaning duties. Lori wiped her hands on her apron and walked to the door. As she reached for the gate she heard a loud thud then screamed. Her loud shrill caused him to turn towards the door. Five men rushed in all with guns in tow.

"What in the hell is going on out here?" Jerry yelled as he came running from his office. He stopped dead in his tracks when he realized why his wife was screaming. He knew he had a gun in the office, but hell, what good could his one gun do in there especially when they had five guns out here? He had to think quickly to save his family.

"Where the money at old man?" the biggest out of the group asked.

"Please, please don't hurt my family," Jerry pleaded.

One of the men had Lori by the hair and a gun pointed at her head. She cried and cried but her eyes never left her husbands. The largest man ran over to Jerry and put the gun in his mouth.

"Where the fuck is the money?" he said through clenched teeth.

Jerry pointed to the back. The large man ordered one of his men to go crank up the car while one was the lookout and another had Bryce on the ground face down. The last man was still holding poor Lori at gunpoint.

"I'm about to take this nigga to the back and get this money. Y'all hold it down out here," the man said as he walked to the back pointing his gun at the back of Jerry's head the whole time.

All of a sudden, Carmesha came out of the kitchen catching everyone off guard.

"What's going on mama?" she said as she entered the room. But before she could even register what was happening, the lookout by the door shot her, startled by her sudden entrance.

"NO!" Lori screamed.

Bryce tried to get up.

"Nigga, I will spray your brains all over this floor. Don't fucking move," said the gunman that had him on the floor as he pressed his gun into Bryce's head.

Lori wouldn't stop screaming and crying as she watched the blood from her daughter's lifeless body, stain the carpet. The big man came from the back, voice booming with authority.

"What the fuck is going on out here?" he asked.

"Aye nigga, watch yo back!" the man holding Lori hostage yelled and started shooting. Jerry had run from his office firing his gun. He hit the big man in the arm before bullets ripped his entire midsection apart. He dropped his gun and was dead before he even hit the ground. Lori screamed even louder.

"Bitch, I told you to shut the fuck up damn!" the man yelled and shot her in the back of the head. He reached

into her apron and pulled out a stack of money. He eyed it for a minute before stuffing it in his pockets. Sirens could be heard in the distance. He dashed out of the door followed by the lookout. The big man ran back into the office and grabbed as much money as he could out of the open safe.

"Nigga hurry up!" said the dude that had Bryce held at gunpoint. He still had the gun to his head. The big man sprinted out of the office and made a beeline for the door.

"Come on, leave that little nigga there," he said while running out the door. He wanted to shoot him so that he could say he shot someone too; he had stripes to earn. The man hesitated for only a second and the bathroom door swung open. Shot's came out of nowhere startling both Bryce and the gunman. Bryce thought he had been shot until he felt the weight of the dead body that had just fell on his back. He felt someone push the dead body off him. He looked up and although he didn't know the man standing before him, he knew that he would be forever indebted to him. The man reached out and helped him on his feet.

"Police! Police! Put your fucking hands in the air," said a swarm of cops as they entered the room.

Both Bryce and the mystery man were taken down for questioning then released after they were ruled out as suspects. Bryce went straight home and stayed in his room for an entire week. He only emerged when it was time to bury his family. As he sat at the funeral staring at his family in their coffins, he was overcome with grief and began to cry. He couldn't believe that this had happened to him. His uncle, aunt, and cousin were all dead. He would have been dead too if it hadn't been for the stranger that had come from the bathroom blasting, and just in the nick of time. He happened to be at the funeral but Bryce was too distraught to acknowledge him.

A week after the funeral he was still having a difficult time coming to terms with what had happened to his family. He felt guilty because his family died in front of him and he did nothing to try to stop it. In a week's time though, he had learned that the big man in charge was a man named Kane from Anderson. Of course, the police didn't know this information, but the streets talked. Bryce swore to his family that he wouldn't rest until he put Kane in the ground.

Bryce hit his fist on the dashboard. Damn! He hated thinking about that shit, but how could he ever forget.

Finding out that Kane was behind Charese's threats and Courtni's kidnapping, only added fuel to the fire.

Chapter Twenty

Charese was bathing Courtni in the tub. They were in Belton safe and sound with Bryce and his thug ass friends. Charese had never seen any shit like that before. Courtni refused to go to the hospital so Charese made it her personal duty to take care of her. They were both silent. Courtni was wondering how she would cope in the days to come and Bryce had left Charese wondering what he was thinking about that made him hit the dashboard so angrily earlier.

"Will you grab a towel for me?" Courtni weakly requested.

"Sure, no problem," Charese said as she jumped up and retrieved a towel from the linen closet. She helped Courtni out of the tub and on to the king size bed in the bedroom. She cried as she dried her off and doctored her wounds.

"Reesy, I told myself that I would never forgive you for this but then I figured that would be selfish with me. After all, you didn't have to come for me."

Charese just looked at her through teary eyes and grabbed her as they held each other close.

"I thought I had lost you too," Charese said thinking about her cousin Porsche.

"I love you girl," Courtni said.

"I love you too," Charese said and meant it. Courtni was more like her sister than her best friend. Just as Charese was about to ask how it happened there was a knock at the door.

"You decent Courtni?" Bryce asked through the door.

"Come on in," she answered.

He walked in with soup, juice, and a grilled cheese sandwich on a tray. He set the tray on the nightstand beside the bed.

"Here's something to put on your stomach," he said trying not to stare.

"I appreciate the effort, but I haven't had anything real to eat in days. Can I get some Waffle House or something?" she asked and managed to smile.

"I can make that happen," he said with a chuckle. Then his tone got serious. "Look though, in all seriousness y'all are going to have to lay low with me for a little while and do whatever I say. Shit about to get real out here. I gave that mothafucka some counterfeit money so I know shit about to be popping in these streets."

Charese looked at him wide eyed.

"Don't look at me like that mama, I told you I wasn't giving up that kind of money," Bryce scolded.

"So what do you want us to do?" she asked.

"Y'all gonna have to go to Charlotte with Seven and Dub. Champ is gonna stay behind with me.

"Charlotte!" Charese shrieked.

"Yes Reesy," he confirmed grabbing her by the shoulders. "It's gonna get crazy around here and I don't need y'all getting hurt or worse. Don't worry about shit or packing shit. My boys got y'all. Y'all are gonna leave around 5."

Charese interrupted him, "Tonight?" she asked.

"Yea, and y'all not coming back until I say so."

"Damn," was all that she could say.

"I'm serious Reesy," he warned.

"Okay," she said lowering her eyes to the floor. Shit was getting crazier by the minute.

Courtni remained silent and looked completely lost; she wasn't built for this life. Bryce told them to get some rest and he left the room. Courtni curled up into a fetal position and fell asleep.

Chapter Twenty-One

Bryce left Seven in charge of taking care of the girls. Dub was tagging along for extra security and Champ's crazy ass was staying behind with Bryce and Kat. Seven was a big man and could handle any man by himself. He was kind of upset that he was being sent to Charlotte, but he knew that Bryce was right when he said the girls needed the best protection and who better to give that to them than him? He was loyal to be Bryce and had been since the tragic night when they met.

He had been in the bathroom drunk and unable to move. He knew that he had been in there for over an hour. When he finally felt that he was able to move he heard all of the commotion on the other side of the door. He crept to the door and slowly cracked it open trying to be as inconspicuous as possible. His eyes couldn't believe what they saw. He just had to get drunk and end up in the middle of a fucking robbery. He instinctively reached for his pistol, but knew that it was useless. They had five guns out there, maybe more. When the last gunman was left alone he saw that as his only chance. He swung the door open and started emptying his clip. He didn't miss the surprised look on either of their faces as he watched the dead gunman fall on top of his hostage. He heard police sirens getting closer in the background. He knew it was only a matter of time before someone called the police; they were in a neighborhood after all. He walked out of the bathroom and pushed the dead man off of the other man and helped him stand to his feet.

"Police! Police! Put your fucking hands in the air!" said about ten cops as they swarmed into the room.

Both he and the man were taken down for questioning then released after they were ruled out as suspects. He felt bad for the surviving man that night. Especially when he saw the bodies of the lady that cooked those delicious wings, the owner, and the sexy waitress that had fed him beer after beer. He attended the funeral, partially out of respect, but mainly because he came across some valuable information that he wanted to share with the man he had heard was named Bryce. He didn't have a chance to tell him at the funeral because he was so distraught, he had been looking for him in the streets, but he had no luck.

A week later, he was riding past the cemetery and saw Bryce sitting on one of the tombstones with a liquor bottle in his hand. He pulled over, got out of his car, and slowly approached him. He must have startled him because he fell off the tombstone once he realized he had company.

"What's up man? I'm Seven," he said as he introduced himself. He reached down and helped him up off the ground for the second time. He was sloppy drunk. Seven chuckled.

"Don't you think you've had enough man?" he asked.

"Hell nah!" he slurred as he dapped him up, "I'm Bryce bruh," he tried to straighten himself out as he reclaimed his position on the tombstone.

"I'm sorry about your people."

"Don't man," Bryce stopped him. "You saved my life and I saw you at the funeral. I owe you man," his eyes teared up.

"Well look, I got some information that you would love to hear," Seven informed him as he watched him sober up within seconds.

"What's up bruh?" Bryce asked.

"That big nigga that was in charge, his name is Kane, he's from Anderson, on the East Side. Some nigga he fuck wit down here put him on to your uncle's business, told him he could hit a serious lick if he robbed the place. I can't remember his name but he was the lookout. Another nigga named Chris from up there sat in there all night watching the place. When the last customer left so did he. That was the signal for Kane and his boys, who ran in the spot while your aunt was at the door. Kane got about one hundred stacks off your uncle. He's supposed to be opening a strip club up there," he watched the fire ignite in Bryce's eyes and continued on.

"But obviously Chris wasn't watching the place well enough because I was still in the bathroom. I went in there and never came out because I was drunk. Yo, I had you that night and I got you now my nigga," he looked him square in the eye as they dapped each other up.

"You drove?" Bryce asked.

"Yea, what's up?"

"Come on let's go," Bryce said.

Seven didn't say anything until he got in the car. "Where to?" he asked.

"Belton," he said. He got on the phone and started making calls as Seven headed to Belton.

They ended up at Oak Forest apartments. They parked in front of a tall, light-skinned man that was waiting on them in the breezeway. When they got out of the car, he got up and met them.

"Whaddup kid?" the light-skinned man said as they embraced each other.

Bryce's tone was serious. "I need you man."

The light-skinned man handed the blunt he was smoking to Bryce and eyed Seven suspiciously.

"Who this big nigga?" he asked.

"This is my man Seven. He good wit me so he good witchu. Seven, this my nigga Champ right here. Me and this nigga moved up here from Atlanta together. Aye, your sister home?" he asked.

"Hell yea, why you think I'm out here smoking."

"We need to talk man."

Champ looked back at the building then at Bryce and reluctantly said, "Man come on. If she curses me out, that's your ass nigga. I don't wanna hear that shit."

They followed Champ up the stairs and into the apartment. When they walked in, a chocolate nigga with long Bone, Thugs & Harmony hair was watching TV. He eyed Seven, but said what's up to Bryce. Bryce spoke back.

"Nah, I mean what's up man? Who this cat you got in here?" the chocolate man asked.

"Chill, this my man's Seven. Seven, this Dub," Bryce said.

Seven and Dub gave each other the 'what's up nigga' nod. Seven took a seat at the kitchen table that was beside *the door. There was a short, shapely woman in the kitchen cooking. She peeked her head around the corner.*

"What's up Shay?"

She looked at Champ. "Nigga what the fuck I tell you about your damn company, huh? You don't pay bills in here. I'ma send your ass back to Atlanta with mommy," she said.

Champ shot fire with his eyes at Bryce. Bryce threw his hands in the air.

"Man have a seat!" he said as he pushed Bryce towards the kitchen table. "I told your ass she was gonna trip!"

Shay rolled her eyes at her brother as she walked over to Bryce and hugged him tight.

"Sorry about your family," she said with sincerity. Her eyes softened as she looked at him.

"I wanted to pay my respects but my job wouldn't let me off."

"Thanks," was all Bryce said.

She turned and walked back into the kitchen.

"So what's up man?" Champ asked.

Bryce looked at Dub and waved him over. "Man get out that game. I need you over here," he said.

Dub sighed and took the remaining seat at the table. Bryce asked Seven to repeat what he told him earlier.

"Damn, that's fucked up," Champ said

"So that's how that nigga bought that club," Dub said and shook his head.

"So what's up man? What we gonna do?" Champ asked.

Before he could answer, Shay came out of the kitchen and set a plate in front of Dub.

"I'ma tell y'all niggas now, don't bring no bullshit back to my front door. Whatever y'all do leave that shit out there," she said pointing to the door. "And don't come back to my house afterwards either. I can't be goin' to jail for none of y'all niggas; not even you Champ. Y'all can fix yourselves a plate if you're hungry." She walked to the playpen in the corner, picked up her daughter, and walked into the bedroom.

They sat, talked, and plotted for three hours before they finally had a plan. Seven called one of his homeboys and he was on his way, and Bryce called his cousin Kat. Kat was also his right hand. He moved to South Carolina a year after Bryce and Champ did. They planned to reverse the roles on Kane, they were going to run up in his spot and take his money. But Bryce had a secret agenda; he planned on killing Kane and anybody that got in his way. Bryce's phone rang; it was Kat letting him know that he was outside. When Bryce went outside to meet him, he was shocked to see Kat getting out of a brand new Denali.

"Damn nigga, when u cop this shit?" Bryce asked as they embraced, he was impressed.

"Aww, that's just some shit I picked up," Kat quickly answered. "So what's up? Why you call me all the way out here?"

"I need you tonight cuz," Bryce said getting right to the point.

Kat didn't miss the seriousness in his tone.

"You got it cuz, what's up?" he asked.

"I found out some nigga named Kane was behind the shit that happened to Uncle Jerry and them. Me and my boys gettin at that nigga tonight!"

Kat looked like he had seen a ghost.

"What's wrong man?" Bryce asked.

"Nothing, I'm good," Kat answered brushing him off.

"Well come on then," Bryce said playfully, punching him in the arm as they walked up the stairs to the apartment. Bryce was close to Kat; they were first cousins, their uncle Jerry was both of their mother's big brother. They walked in and Bryce introduced Kat to

Seven and Dub. Seven eyed Kat; it was something about him that was familiar. He eyed everything from his posture to the nervous look in his eyes. He'd seen it somewhere, but couldn't remember where. He let it go telling himself that it would come to him later.

"We gotta go to the spot and load up," Champ said

They all got up to leave and began load up on guns and ammunition then headed to Anderson. Bryce's adrenaline was rushing as he thought of how good he would feel after he killed Kane. Dub parked the big Tahoe that they were in behind the building. The parking lot was empty with the exception of two cars so they went unnoticed. Bryce was in the passenger's seat putting the silencer on his .9mm. Kat was in the backseat sweating bullets.

Bryce looked at him. "Aight cuz, just go in there and act like you're lost. We're coming in right behind you," he instructed.

Kat took a deep breath then got out of the car. Bryce and his goons waited until Kat opened the door to the building before they got out and followed his lead.

Chapter Twenty-Two

Kane and Chris were sitting on the stage of his new club counting money. The club's grand opening was set for the following weekend. Chris was looking around in admiration.

"This shit gonna be tight!" he complimented.

"Yea, I'ma call it Fantasy!" Kane said as he laughed out loud. He paused then looked at Chris.

"Thanks for your help man," he said. Chris knew he was talking about the robbery without him even having to say it. He didn't think that things would go down the way they did and he was remorseful. It seemed as if he was the only one that had a conscience, Kane and his homeboys didn't give a fuck and the nigga that set it up was just trying to cover his ass.

"Hey man, you hooked me up," Chris said while eyeing the watch that he had bought with his portion of the money.

Kane smiled.

"I gotta go pick my baby mama up from work," he said as he got up to leave. He dapped Kane up then headed towards the door. As soon as he reached it, it swung open alarming him. When the man walked through the door he

smiled with recognition. Had it been someone trying to kill him, he would have been dead because he thought that he had locked the door behind him when he came in. Kane's gun was in his office, but he wasn't worried once he saw who it was that walked through the door.

"What's up nigga?" Kane said.

Before anything else could be said the door swung open and five niggas ran in.

"What the fuck?" said a shocked and surprised Chris.

"Shut the fuck up nigga," Champ said to Chris as he pointed his gun at him.

He looked at Bryce who took charge by pointing his gun at Kane who was still on stage and Seven's homeboy followed suit.

"Get your ass on the ground," Bryce ordered.

Without his gun he was defenseless, so Kane did as he was told. Seven looked Chris up and down.

"I think this nigga was there that night, B!" Seven exclaimed.

Bryce got angry and was ready to pull the trigger, but Seven told him not to.

"Not until we get what we came here for," Seven reminded him.

Bryce knew that he was right. He looked at Chris who was menacingly staring at Kat. Champ hit Chris in the neck with the butt of his gun and he fell to the floor gasping for air.

"Get your ass up nigga," Champ said. He walked him to where Kane was and made him get on his knees beside him.

Bryce walked up to Kane, "What's up nigga? Checkmate," he said.

Kane smirked; he was unfazed even with a gun pointed at his head.

"Nigga, what the fuck you want from me?" Kane asked.

"Your life, but I'll take that later," Bryce said arrogantly.

Chris pointed at Kat then turned to Bryce, "You dumb motherfucker. This nigga right here" POW! That was all he got out before Kat shot him in the face. Brain matter sprayed the walls as Chris fell back and died leaning against the wall. "Damn nigga!" Champ yelled caught off guard by the sound of the gun.

Bryce didn't flinch; he kept his gun pointed at Kane. "Fuck this nigga. Champ, you and Kat tear this place up. I'ma go to this safe, Seven, you handle that nigga. Bryce walked to the back and was ecstatic when he discovered the already open safe. He stuffed his duffle bag with as much money as he could, then his pockets.

He heard Seven say, "Fill her up and don't try no funny shit," just as he was walking out of Kane's office.

"Yea, put all my people money in there," he said as he watched Kane grab the bag and fill it with the money that was on the stage.

Kane kept eyeing Kat. Kat started sweating profusely, anyone with eyes could tell he was nervous. Bryce was equally nervous; he had never taken a life before.

Kane handed Seven the bag while still staring at Kat. Kane opened his mouth to speak.

"Shut the fuck up nigga before you be stretched out beside your homeboy," Kat said before Kane could even get a word out.

Seven handed the bag to Dub and he and his homeboy took the two bags of money outside. Seven took a bag out of his back pocket and filled it with the remaining money that was left on the stage. Bryce looked at Kane and without a second thought he shot him three times. He took his jewelry, all of his money out of his pockets and socks, and even his shoes. Seven, Kat, and Bryce went through the club and grabbed whatever guns and bullets they could find. They all ran out and piled into the truck and took off en route to Dub's mother's house.

Once they got there and everyone had their nerves intact, they counted the money. They had a little over one hundred and fifty thousand dollars. Bryce gave each of his boy's twenty stacks and kept the rest for himself. He was going to spend half of his money on himself the rest was on drugs. He was trying to come up on a come up.

"So what now?" Kat asked.

Bryce pulled out a bag of loud and a White Owl Silver from his pocket and began to roll up.

"I'm about to come up," he said as he looked at each of them, "and I'm taking y'all with me."

Seven stared at Kat; it was something about him that just didn't sit right with him. He couldn't shake the feeling that he saw him somewhere but still couldn't place his face.

Seven snapped out of his daze and shook his head a lot of shit had changed since then. But he and Bryce were still cool and he still didn't trust Kat. He acted very suspicious to him but he wasn't going to say anything to Bryce until he could figure out where he saw him before. He walked into the bedroom and lightly shook Charese awake.

"Reesy, wake up. It's time to move," Seven said gently.

She got up and woke Courtni up so she could help her get ready. Once they were ready, Seven carried Courtni to the car.

"Can we stop and get something to eat?" Charese asked

"Yea, once we get on the road," he answered.

Silence engulfed them as they neared Highway 85. Courtni drifted off to sleep and Charese remained silent as she stared out the window thinking about how much her life had changed in such little time. She missed Taye and Tip and was worried about her Aunt Kathy. She was done with Tee. Out of all the bitches in the world to cheat on her with and he chose Shi Shi's nasty ass. Eventually Charese joined Courtni and she drifted off into a deep slumber.

Chapter Twenty-Three

When Charese woke up, they were taking exit 33 in Charlotte. Dub pulled into a Chick-Fil-A drive thru and they ordered breakfast. Then rode around on Billy Graham Parkway to Tyron Blvd. to Tyvola Street. Charese wanted to stay at the Hilton, but Seven insisted on the Howard Johnson. Courtni insisted that she eat at the IHOP that was in front of the hotel. They got their food and by the time they checked in, it was almost eight am.

Once they entered the room Seven said, "Y'all can sleep in that bed, Dub, you take the one closest to the window, and I'll take the chair by the door."

Charese didn't say a word as she grabbed two Tylenol PM's, fixed a cup of ice water and handed them to Courtni who took them and laid down.

"So what are we supposed to do now?" Charese asked.

"Don't ask any questions. We got this," that was Dub. Seven looked at him sideways which made him shut up and go back to eating his food. His gaze softened as he returned his attention back to Charese.

"Well for starters you're going to get some rest pretty lady and stop worrying so much. Later we're gonna catch some lunch then I will take y'all to get some clothes because I don't know how long we're going to be here.

The rest is up to B," he said as he gave her a playful hug that made her smile.

She let out an exasperated sigh and laid down beside Courtni planning on joining her in la la land. Dub turned on the TV and turned it up loud while he flipped through the channels. Ever since this shit went down, he's had a nasty attitude towards her and she was tired of it so she asked him what his problem was.

"A nigga tired man, I had to leave my ole' lady and my daughter just to come babysit y'all."

Charese flipped, "You ugly motherfucker I didn't ask for your help! You ain't got no muscle anyway, you're a runner!" she yelled.

Seven laughed, she didn't, Dub didn't find it too funny either and Courtni was sound asleep.

Charese was on a roll, "What does Bryce use you for anyway? You're a casualty nigga!"

Dub looked like he wanted to smack Charese and Seven couldn't do anything but laugh.

Seven looked at Dub, "What's up man? You're not fuckin wit the fam no more?" he asked.

Dub gave him a 'you know me better than that' look.

"Man, fuck him and all that shit he's talking about," Charese said. She was annoyed and so over Dub's attitude. She reached into her purse and pulled out a pack of White Owl cigars. She went to the trashcan and dissected the tobacco guts from the cigar before returning to the bed. She laid her empty cigar on the nightstand and began filling it up with that good shit.

"Lil' Reesy, you smoke?" asked a surprised Seven.

She nodded as she wrapped her lips around the cigar paper; she lit it and hit it until a calming sensation took over her body. She passed it to Seven, as they passed it around, Courtni shot up from her pillow.

"That shit smell like some gas! Let me hit it," she said and they all burst out laughing, even Dub.

They chilled and sat around doing nothing all day, which was driving everyone crazy, eventually, everyone fell asleep. Charese was the first to wake up and was shocked to see that it was seven the next morning. She looked at Seven who looked very uncomfortable trying to sleep in that little chair; she laughed and woke him up.

"Let's go get some breakfast," she suggested.

He yawned loudly while stretching then looked at her and smiled.

"I haven't woken up to beauty in a while," he said making her blush.

They woke Courtni and Dub up and they all walked to IHOP for breakfast. Charese wasn't speaking to Dub; she was done with him. He sat alone trying to mack to a waitress that was on break and both Courtni and Charese sat with Seven. He told Charese how he and Bryce met after she promised not to repeat it. To say that she was shocked was an understatement.

After they ate, they rode to the South Park Mall to go shopping. They had valet parking at the mall and Charese was amazed, she'd never saw anything like it before. They each got about a week's worth of clothing before returning to their room. Bryce called to talk to Seven then asked to speak to Charese. He told her that he was gonna lay low for a minute and he loved her. She was in shock because she had yet to sort out her feelings and she told him that.

He changed the subject and told her that he sent word to their families that they were safe so they wouldn't worry. Charese laughed as Bryce told her that Taye hemmed him up at Burger King asking about her and Courtni. She didn't ask, but he told her that he hadn't seen Tee since the day she caught him with Shi Shi. He promised that it would be over soon and ended the call. Charese cried herself to sleep.

Seven was staring out the window thinking about all the shit that had happened. Then, for some reason, he started thinking about the robbery that started it all in Greenwood. He replayed everything he saw that night while hiding in the bathroom. Then he remembered,

He sat straight up in his chair. "Kat!" he yelled startling everyone out of their sleep.

"What?" Charese and Dub asked in unison.

"Aww shit! I knew it was something about that nigga!" Seven said ignoring them as he picked up his phone and called Bryce.

Chapter Twenty-Four

Kane was sitting in his office with two of his runners counting his money. He was fifty thousand dollars richer and thinking about opening another club. He had more than enough money to do it. Hell, he could open up two more clubs if he wanted to. His new head bitch was giving him head while he tended to his business. She wasn't as good as Toya, but she would suffice. Damn, he missed Toya; that was his little shooter. He felt some type of way towards her for killing his seed though. He still couldn't believe that she killed Porsche, the best piece of pussy he had ever had in his whole thirty years of life.

What he really couldn't believe was that the delusional bitch thought he was gonna wait around for twenty years until she got out of prison. Ha! He didn't even wait two days. Don't act surprised, y'all know what it is when you're dealing with a thug, a real street nigga. All of a sudden one of his boys took a twenty out of his wallet and held it next to the twenty he was counting. The glow that the twenty he was counting was not on the twenty from his pocket, which caught Kane's attention. The dude looked at Kane as he eyed the money. Everyone was silent for all of five minutes before Kane smacked the money on the floor scaring the hell out of Sparkle who jumped.

"Bitch get out," he told her.

She stopped giving him head and ran out of the room. Kane let out an angry roar that frightened the other men in the room. He replayed the money exchange over again in his head. Then his thought drifted to the little nigga that was in charge, the one that Charese was all over. What stood out was the way he looked at Kane. It was something about the look he had on his face. It was the same look he had on his face at IHOP and the same look he had in his office! The fucking busboy from the liquor house robbery!

This nigga got some balls! Kane thought to himself. Then he remembered that night at the club. He should have put two and two together when he said, "get all my people money.". And that nigga Kat? He was definitely gonna get what he deserved. He thought about the night they robbed him. They killed his right hand man, Chris, then took him to the back and shot him too and left him for dead. But they didn't check to make sure he was dead before they left. They didn't even check to see if he had a pulse! After they left he crawled to his desk and called 911. So when word got around that he survived and still had money to blow, he blew up. He was what you would call "Hood Famous" He started busting niggas heads at the door to make up for his loss; he had come up real quick. He looked at his boys and said,

"These niggas want to start a war wit me!" he yelled then threw a stack of hundreds at the wall.

*****

Bryce started to think that he was in over his head. He wasn't really a killer, but Kane had brought out a beast in him. He was about getting money, but he knew if he didn't kill Kane, Kane would kill him. He was in a fucked up situation. He was at his aunt's house in Greenwood; he didn't plan on staying long because he didn't want to put her in any danger. He was about to call Champ when his phone rang. He thought it was Charese because she had grown impatient. They had been in Charlotte for two weeks and she and Courtni were ready to come home.

"Hello," he answered.

"Aye man!" it was Kat.

"Whaddup cuz?" Bryce asked him.

"Shit done hit the fan," Kat told him.

Bryce sat up, "What's going on?" he questioned.

"Kane said come to the club tonight with two kilos of coke or he gonna kill me man," he said. The line went silent then he heard Kane's voice at the other end of the line.

"Don't play wit me homeboy or I'll drop this fake ass nigga where he stand!" Kane threatened before he hung up.

"Shit!" Bryce yelled. He didn't have any other choice but to give Kane the drugs. He couldn't let him kill his cousin. He called Champ and told him what was up; he knew shit would get real once Kane realized he tricked him with counterfeit money.

Later that night, Bryce found himself in the basement of Club Fantasy. Kane was accompanied by two other men. They had Kat tied to a chair and he looked mortified.

"You thought that shit was clever didn't you? You got my work nigga?" Kane asked.

Bryce threw a suitcase with the drugs in it at Kane. Just then, his phone rung but he ignored the call. Kane opened the suitcase and smiled. He reached in his pocket and pulled out a knife. He cut a small slit in one of the packs; putting just a little bit on his index finger to sample the product. He pointed his finger at Bryce showing off his pearly whites.

"This some good shit. Like some straight off the boat type shit!" Kane stated clearly impressed.

Champ's phone rung and he answered it, "Hello."

"Get the fuck off the phone," Kane said.

"Nigga shut the fuck up. This is my shit! Your business right there," Champ said pointing to the suitcase sitting in front of Kane.

Bryce chuckled.

One of Kane's boys shifted his weight and Kane held his hand up, signaling for him to stand down.

"Nigga you lying! Do you know where the fuck we at right now?" Champ yelled into his phone.

By this time, Kane wanted to know what was going on, as did Bryce, but he refused to take his eyes off Kane.

Dub ended his call and looked at Kat. "So how much Kane pay you to set your own people up?" he asked.

Bryce looked at Kat horrified, praying that he had heard Champ wrong.

"Answer the motherfucking question nigga," Champ demanded.

Kane was grinning from ear to ear and Kat just stared at Bryce. It sickened Bryce to his stomach.

"B," Kat started to say.

"You were in on Uncle Jerry's murder?" Bryce asked rhetorically, barely above a whisper.

"B," Kat repeated himself.

"If it's any consolation, he flipped on me too the night y'all robbed me," Kane said. He paused and looked at Kat. "Wait, that's why you shot Chris, because he was about to tell your little secret!" He hit Kat in the head with a chair causing blood to pour from the back of his head.

Bryce was speechless; everything made sense to him now. Before he knew it, he reached for his gun, aimed it at Kat and pulled the trigger. Because he was tied to a chair, Kat was defenseless against the bullets as they tore into his chest and abdomen. He tried to say I'm sorry, but the only thing that came out of his mouth was blood before he took his final breath.

Kane took that as his cue. He grabbed the suitcase and started running, shooting aimlessly at Bryce and Champ. Kane's boys started shooting at them in an attempt to protect Kane, but Champ quickly ended one of their lives with a clean shot between the eyes and Bryce shot the other in the neck. Champ started shooting while running to the exit behind Kane but the time they made it outside, Kane was speeding out of the parking lot. Bryce started shooting at the Infiniti causing the innocent bystanders to scatter in fear. They hopped in the car and took off before the police were called.

"Shit, shit, SHIT!" Bryce screamed as he repeatedly punched the window.

Chapter Twenty-Five

Seven was worried about Bryce, as was Charese. It had been two weeks and they had yet to hear from him. He spoke with Dub briefly who informed him that Bryce had killed Kat. Seven told him it had been bothering since he met Kat at his girlfriend's house. Damn that's dirty. Charese was extremely worried about Bryce. She had already put so much on his plate so she knew he didn't have room for anything else. Dub informed them that he hadn't heard from Bryce either.

"Man fuck this, I gotta go see about my mans," Seven said out of nowhere by the end of the third week.

Charese jumped up. "I was wondering when you were gonna come to your senses," she said.

He smiled at her. "You alright with me lil' Reesy," he said.

They all packed their things and within forty-five minutes, they were back on the highway headed to Anderson. They all tried calling Bryce the entire time, but all they ever got was the voicemail.

Once they arrived in Anderson, Seven dropped everyone off. Charese walked Courtni inside of her home and made sure all was well. She cried as she apologized to her family and explained everything.

Seven dropped Reesy off last. She thanked and hugged him.

"When are we gonna start looking for Bryce?" she asked.

"You can't come with me right now, I gotta figure out what's going on. But if you need me, you call me Reesy," he said looking into her eyes.

"Thank you," she said as she exited the car. She walked in the house and was surprised to see Aunt Kathy sitting on the couch. It looked like she had been crying and when she saw Charese she started crying again. She hugged Charese as they both cried then suddenly she smacked her.

"Where the hell have you been?" she asked.

Holding her face, Charese stood there in shock. Aunt Kathy looked at her and shook her head. She retired to her bedroom where she remained for the rest of the night. Charese showered, put on some pajamas, and then stretched out on the couch. She flipped through the channels and decided to watch Golden Girls. She took a box of chocolate ice cream out of the freezer, grabbed a spoon and continued watching TV.

Five days later, she was still trying to reach Bryce but was still getting his voicemail. She couldn't even leave him a message because his voicemail was full. She wasn't sure what to think at this point; it had been almost a month. She talked to Tee once, but it was a very strained conversation. The tension was so thick that he made up a lame excuse to get off the phone; she didn't care one way or the other. They both knew that their relationship was over. She had also spoken to Taye and Tip briefly. They both wanted to see her, but she wasn't up for any company. Tip was upset and not very understanding, so Charese decided to leave her alone for a while.

She didn't need Tip and her emotions complicating things. Aunt Kathy was barely speaking to her, but she was about to move anyway. She still had the money that Bryce had given her. She saw a house on Belton Avenue and another on South Fant Street and both were for rent. She called and left messages with both realtors so hopefully she would get one. She was really upset that Bryce still hadn't returned any of her calls. Maybe he grew tired of her and her drama, but she didn't ask him to be her Superman. Or maybe he was dead. No, she refused to even entertain that thought. Seven still hadn't been able to find him, but had called to check on her. She was grateful for him. They were becoming really good friends.

Chapter Twenty-Six

Seven, Dub, and Champ were all out riding around looking for Bryce. They left no stone unturned and there was still no sign of him. It had been a month since Bryce disappeared and shit was in chaos. They had gotten into it with Kane and his goons on several occasions. Although none of them had gotten hurt, they killed two of Kane's men. They didn't know what to do and now they were fighting amongst each other. Champ was a real nigga, but he knew when he was in over his head. He wanted to squash the beef with Kane so they wouldn't have to worry about losing their lives every time they walked the streets. But at the same time he thought he understood what Bryce was going through.

Bryce wasn't built for this life. He was the get money nigga, Seven was the muscle, Dub was the thugged out one, and he was the hothead. Even though Bryce was his boy, Dub was feeling the same way. The way he figured, Bryce didn't give a fuck about what happened to them or else he would be right there fighting, shooting, and killing right along with them and they wouldn't be looking for him. Shit, Bryce was MIA, he had to look out for himself and Champ, because Shay would kill him if he let something happen to her little brother.

Now Seven, he wasn't hearing any of that. Bryce was his man and he was going to be loyal until the end. But he'd be lying to himself if he said Dub didn't have a point. Hell, he had a daughter, Khamari, to live for. Bryce wasn't worried about them or what they had been through in the past couple of weeks. Kane didn't intimidate him in the least, but he knew the odds we stacked up against them. Bryce had created a mess then left them to clean up behind him. Seven was more worried than upset. Bryce had a lot on his plate, Seven knew it was only a matter of time before his boy broke down. He just needed to talk to him.

*****

Bryce was confused, hurt, and angry all at the same time. Kat was his first cousin. Kat's mother was the youngest of their grandmother's children. He just couldn't wrap his mind around the fact that his own flesh and blood betrayed him like that. Betrayed his family, and for that reason, he deserved to die. Now that he knew the truth, it seemed like everything was coming together and he ignored all of the signs. Kat didn't go to the funerals. Seven had been looking at him sideways since the moment he introduced the two, Kane and his homeboy Chris had been giving Kat the same exact looks. Kane was right. Kat shot and killed Chris because he was about to expose him for the snake that he was.

Damn, he hated that things had to go down the way that they did. Then to top it all off, he was unsure of what to do about the whole situation. He wasn't a thug; he was in over his head. He was at home, at the house that no one knew about; not even his boys. He was having mixed emotions. He had been there since the night he murdered his cousin. The whole time, he refused to talk to anybody until he came to terms with himself. He entertained the thought of taking his money and hightailing it to Cancun or somewhere and never looking back, but he knew better. He knew he couldn't leave his boys or Charese hanging like that.

He knew they were all out looking for him, but he also knew that he created a monster; the monster being the situation that they were currently in. He had never been involved in anything like this and if someone would have told him five years ago that he would be, he would not have believed them. He knew eventually that he would have to come out of his shell and return to the streets. He would have to return to Charese, he loved her. He had to love her to allow so much drama into his life just to get next to her. When it was all over, and he survived, he was going to marry her and get them out of the hood for good.

Chapter Twenty-Seven

TWO MONTHS LATER

Charese was sitting in her Accounting class when her financial aid officer pulled her out. After everything that she had been through, she still managed to start school on time, which was exactly what she needed. She was going to have to get a job to cover what financial aid didn't pay for. She moved away so she was going to have to rebuild her clientele. She was going to use her hair money for bills. She moved to Gateway Village, an apartment complex in Simpsonville, SC, which was almost an hour away from Anderson.

She kept to herself and no one bothered her. It was very quiet and completely dead. There wasn't any kind of action going on, but that's the kind of peace she needed. She had to cut Tip off as a lover and a friend. She told her that she just wanted to be friends without the clit rubbing and Tip went ballistic. She was on some crazy, stalker type shit. Everywhere she went there was Tip. She was still cool with Courtni and Taye though.

She was okay in Simpsonville. Her mind was at ease and she made a little bit of money. She handed out "Styles by Nicole" business cards, using her middle name just as a precaution. She had a few select Anderson clients come to her home to get their hair done. These were the people she knew that she could trust not to tell anyone her whereabouts. She didn't know if anything would happen to her in Anderson but she sure wasn't going to stick around to find out.

She got the house on Belton Ave but decided against it, thinking it would be best to just leave Anderson. She heard from Courtni that Bryce was still nowhere in sight and that Seven and Champ paid Kane off to squash the beef so they weren't trying to kill each other anymore. She wanted to reach out to Seven but realized she lost his number after she had already thrown her phone away and gotten a new one. She wondered if he had at least heard from Bryce. She wanted to go ride around and see what she could find out, but she was still terrified of Anderson. These were the thoughts that were going through her head as her financial aid officer told her what she already knew. She was going to have to find a job and soon.

After the bad news, she was done with Greenville Tech for the day so she decided to go home. She copped a gram of loud from her neighbor and entered her apartment. After eating and taking a shower, she flopped down on the couch and called Courtni. She was working at a shop now and doing better. She told Charese that there was a booth open and she should rent it. Courtni was trying desperately to get her girl to come back home. If anybody should be scared, it should be her, but Charese wasn't having that. Courtni kept assuring her that everything would be okay, but Charese was just not convinced. And if she came home, it would be to work for herself; she still refused to work in anybody's shop.

Business had picked up a little, but without a job, she was going to have to quit school. Things were finally looking up for her. She missed Bryce but he had completely abandoned her. He may as well have played her like Tee and Trap because all three had let her down in some way or another. She was just at a loss and didn't know what to do. She missed Anderson but she didn't wanna go home and have to look over her shoulders every five minutes. She didn't know if Kane would come after her or not, but she didn't care to find out. Courtni could be right, but then again, she couldn't read that man's mind. He wanted her dead and there was nothing she could do about it. She showered then got ready for bed.

The next morning Charese awoke determined to find a job or some kind of come up. She got dressed then left for school. Her mind wasn't even focused as she sat in sociology class thinking of ways that she could come up with some fast money. After she left class she headed to the financial aid office. She gave them the money she had left over from what Bryce had given her, but of course it still wasn't enough. Thank God she had already paid up her rent for the whole year and her car was paid off or she would have been headed straight up shit's creek without a paddle.

If she had to continue living off oodles of noodles and hot pockets then so be it. She decided that she was just going to give up looking for Bryce. She had to look out for herself because all she had was herself. She walked into the financial aid office only to be told that her request to borrow access funds had been denied. She walked out in the middle of the conversation. There was nothing more she could do; she was going to have to drop out.

She left school and went to Wendy's. Although she tried her best to keep her composure, she was in tears before she sat down with her Jr. Cheeseburger meal. She could feel the stares of everyone around her but she didn't care. A lady gave her some napkins; she thanked her as she wiped her face. She picked at her food for a while then just sat there staring out the window. She felt someone run their fingers through her hair, which was now short.

"Aww Reesy, it can't be that bad," she heard a man's voice say.

She turned around and there stood Kane; the look on her face was priceless. She was just as terrified as she was speechless. He took a seat beside her.

"Why don't you tell big daddy Kane what's wrong," he said with a smirk.

She hated him.

"So this is where you ran off too, huh," he said. He waited for a response but she didn't give him one.

"You scared? You think I'm gonna hurt you? Nah, not my sweet, chocolate, Reesy Cup," he said while rubbing his fingers down her back.

She cringed.

"Now tell me what the problem is."

She thought about her money situation. *He could help me* she thought to herself. *Nah, I couldn't get involved with him.* Especially after everything she had been through because of him.

He pulled out a stack of money. She couldn't take her eyes off it.

"Will this solve your problems?" he asked with a sinister grin.

She eyed the money.

"Come on let's talk about it," he grabbed her by the hand and she silently followed. She couldn't believe she was going anywhere with him, but she needed the money. She really, really needed that money.

Chapter Twenty-Eight

Charese stared at herself in the mirror. She looked at her ruffled hair and tear stained face and cried some more. She needed that money so she slept with Kane. She thought of Bryce and her cousin Porsche the entire time. Porsche was the reason she felt guilty; she felt as if she betrayed her, but she needed that money. She walked into her bedroom and stared at the money that was spread across her bed. It was the money she got from Kane; it was enough to get her through two semesters. She was experiencing a myriad of emotions. She hated that she did it, but it seemed like it was her only option. She needed the money like yesterday and working in somebody's shop wasn't going to get it fast enough.

Now she was going to have to start working at Fantasy to keep herself up. She and Kane made an agreement. She was allowed to keep all of her earnings as long as he had unlimited access to the pussy. She took a shower and scrubbed her body like there was no tomorrow. It was like she was dirtier than normal because of what she had just done. She hated the fact that she slept with Kane. What she hated even more was how her body had betrayed her. She came when Kane fucked her and she came hard. She put her money up then laid down and cried herself to sleep.

The next morning she woke up and called her girls. She told Courtni and Taye that she would be coming back to Anderson. They were ecstatic until she told them that she'd be working at Fantasy. They protested but she didn't want to hear their mouths, they weren't paying her bills. Her plan was to find a place back home and start working on the following Friday. She would work on the weekends and go to school during the week. She wasn't giving up her apartment though.

Her phone went off. It was a text message from Kane telling her that the sex was good and he would be back sooner than later. She replied with okay then laid across her bed and stared at the ceiling. Bryce crossed her mind but she quickly blocked any thoughts of him out of her head. She had to move on.

The next week she started getting everything in order. She had slept with Kane twice since their first encounter and she hated that she enjoyed it. She now understood how he had Porsche hooked. She had managed to find a house on Nardin Ave. and that's where she would be staying on the weekends. The house wasn't much, but she didn't plan on keeping it long anyway. As she drove to her new home, she began to cry. She hated the situation that she was in, but she needed the money. Her mind wandered from Bryce to Porsche to Tee to Kane. After everything she'd been through, she still hadn't come up.

Once she reached the house she sat in the parking lot and just stared at it. *This is just until I finish school* she told herself. She brought a blow up mattress, a few pots and pans, toiletries, a few snacks, and a futon for the living room. She looked at the time on her phone; it was five pm. She got out of the car and entered the small one bedroom house. She fixed herself a Marie Callender's microwave dinner then took a shower. After she finished her shower, she rubbed her body down with lotion before she laid across the blow up mattress that she bought from Wal-Mart.

She stared at the outfits she chose, they were modest, but it didn't matter, they wouldn't stay on long anyway. It was going to be her first night at the club and she was a nervous wreck. She grabbed her bag of green and a White Owl from her purse. After she dissected the cigar, she filled it up with the Blue Dream. She lit her L and then laid on her back as the relaxing effects of the marijuana began to take over her, calming her nerves. She wasn't planning on working that many hours. She didn't want to stay in that club longer than she had to.

She eventually drifted off to sleep and was awakened by the sound of her alarm. It was ten pm. She got up, brushed her teeth, changed into a sweat suit then grabbed her bag as she headed out the door. The club was already packed when she arrived. She walked in through the back door and observed her surroundings. She watched women shake their body parts as men watched in lust; she was not ready.

"Reesy? Reesy! What the fuck you doin' in here?" said a male voice.

She turned around to see Tonio staring at her in disbelief as he looked at her gym bag.

"You working here now?" he asked.

She remained silent.

He threw his hands in the air. "Aww come on Reesy, you know you're better than that!"

"Man back up!" she said as she pushed her way past him and headed towards the locker room. When she walked in all eyes were on her and unfortunately, she recognized every face. She ignored the whispers and snickers until one girl said,

"Oh, I know Queen Charese ain't up in here y'all?" Her voice was laced in sarcasm as she high-fived some of the girls.

Charese just stared at her. "Not Miss I'm-the-shit-Charese?" the group erupted in laughter.

Charese ignored them and went to the nearest empty locker. She began to change into her first outfit, but Miss Thang just kept right on talking.

"This bitch must've fell from her throne and realized she a local hoe just like everybody else." She looked at her friends who were all cheering her on.

Charese continued to ignore them. *I'm not gonna let these hoes get to me* she thought. She didn't need friends, attention, or anything. She was just there to collect her coins and head back to Simpsonville. As far as she was concerned, she was done with Anderson. She put on her makeup then her heels.

The same girl said, "I guess we gonna have to show this bitch-" POP! That was all she got out before Charese punched her in the mouth. A crowd gathered around as they watched Charese tear the girl a new asshole. The once animated girl was now as quiet as a mouse, squirming on the floor, praying that someone would break up the fight. Charese beat the girl mercilessly until security finally broke it up. The girl sat up holding her leaking face, but she said nothing. She was just happy to be free.

"What happened to all that mouth you had bitch?" Charese yelled as she got in one last kick, connecting her heel with the side of the girls head, sending her flying back down to the floor.

"Man get off of me!" she started fighting the security until he let her go. She jerked away from the big, burly man. "I'm good," she said.

"Well Kane is gonna wanna see you for this shit," he said with an attitude as he walked out the door.

"Yea okay," she said as she fixed her hair in the mirror and reapplied her lipstick. She looked at the big-mouthed girl who was now being cleaned up by her group of cosigners.

"I'm still that bitch and I'm gonna be that bitch while I'm up in here. Y'all bitches better watch your back because I'm about to take all of your money," she said and walked out the door.

Chapter Twenty-Nine

Charese had been working at the club for a little over a month now and she hated every minute of it. It had been four months since Bryce disappeared on her. She hadn't thought about him in a while but couldn't help but wonder how he was. Her first dance was the most degrading experience of her life. She went by the name Moet because she thought she was 'as fine as wine'. She encountered so many different people, some she didn't want to see but she learned that weed, alcohol, and lots of good sex helped her cope. Kane fed her Ex pills like they were candy and she was hooked. She had been having sex with him every day now. Sometimes up to three times a day and she was thoroughly enjoying it; his sex game was the on point. She was convinced that his dick was magic.

She was on her way to her apartment in Simpsonville. It was a Sunday night, well, Monday morning; it was four am. She was happy because she had made an extra two thousand dollars letting two old white men take turns with her. She hated it, but she had to do it. Now she felt like she was no better than the rest of the strippers. They had sex, gave head, ate each other's pussy, and had threesomes for a quick buck; and so did she.

She was lost and confused, but even more she was ashamed because she enjoyed the feelings she got when she came or when somebody played with her pussy, and it didn't hurt that she was getting paid for it. She got home and unlocked her door. Courtni was on her couch watching Netflix. She had been staying with Charese since she started working at the club.

"Girl, I'm so glad you're home! Where do you keep your tampons?" she asked.

Charese froze.

"Reesy, what's wrong?" Courtni asked as she observed Charese's panicked expression. Charese ran to the kitchen and looked at the calendar.

"No! This can't be life!" she exclaimed.

"Girl, what is going on?" asked a concerned Courtni as she followed Charese into the kitchen.

Charese sat down at the kitchen table.

"Girl, I haven't had a period," she said, barely above a whisper. All of a sudden, her palms were sweaty; so much was going through her head at once. She wasn't sure when her last period was and she had sex with Tee, Bryce, and Kane all without protection. She began to cry.

"Girl calm down, let's just go get a pregnancy test. Maybe it's late because you're stressed," Courtni tried to reassured her.

Charese was silent as she slowly climbed into the passenger's seat. Because she was so emotional, Courtni went in the store to buy the pregnancy test. Charese was quiet all the way home, and even after she peed on the stick. It wasn't until she saw her test results that she spoke.

"Well," Courtni asked.

"Damn," was all Charese could say before she burst into tears.

Courtni helped her get undressed then into bed. She closed the door behind her and gave Charese her privacy.

Charese arose bright and early the next morning and headed to the free clinic that was located near the hospital. She waited impatiently in the nurse's office as she examined the paperwork before her.

"Congratulations Miss Shaw, you are approximately fifteen weeks. It's astonishing that you're not showing this late in your pregnancy. Because we found out so late in the pregnancy we will have to take extra precautions," the nurse was saying.

Unbeknownst to the nurse, she had lost Charese at "fifteen weeks." She took the prenatal vitamins and the little bag of goodies the nurse had given her and stormed out of the office. The nurse was beaming as if it was something to be happy about. She had done so many drugs and fucked so many people; she turned into a real live thot in the past couple of months. What was she gonna do with a baby? And who was the father? That was a better question! She couldn't believe that she had gotten herself in this kind of situation.

She ruled out Kane and any of the club patrons because she wasn't involved with any of them that long ago so that left Tee and Bryce.

Chapter Thirty

Two months had passed since Charese found out that she was with child. Here she was in school, pregnant, and fucking her dead cousin's baby daddy, the man that murdered her possible baby father's family. She did learn, however, that she was carrying a boy. She had always wanted a son, but definitely not under these circumstances. She decided that she was going to give the baby up for adoption; she didn't have a choice. She was in no shape to be anybody's mother; she couldn't even take care of herself right now.

She wanted to find the baby a good loving home. She had already talked it over with Kane and he was going to help her do it, and they were going to do it quietly. She stopped working at the club since learning of her pregnancy. Kane allowed her to stop working so she could keep her pregnancy a secret, but that only meant she had to have more sex with him. He made her do any and everything to him and she hated him for it. She had no choice but to comply; she still needed the money for school. She also needed to save her money because eventually, she planned on getting her son back.

She was in the bathroom bent over the sink, wringing out a washcloth. She wiped the blood from her plump derriere and cried. Kane had come over in a very drunken state and roughly took her ass hole. He pinned her down and choked her, even though she was crying, and told him that he was hurting her stomach; he didn't show an ounce of compassion. After he finished he flipped her over then entered her. He beat and pounded until he came hard inside her. She ran the hot rag over her tear stained face.

"Get your dumb ass out here and cook bitch!" Kane yelled from the living room.

She jumped, terrified at the sound of his voice, and dropped the washcloth on the floor. She had a hard time bending over to pick it up because she was in so much pain and her stomach ached terribly. By the time she managed to reach down and grab it, Kane was standing over her.

"What the fuck is your problem?" he asked.

She was so scared she started to cry once again.

"I'm coming now daddy," she said as she turned to face him. She tried to walk past him, but he grabbed her by her hair. She screamed and he punched her in the mouth immediately drawing blood.

"You a dirty ass club thot!" he said in a menacing tone and hit her in the mouth again.

Her mouth filled with blood and she spit it out. She was whimpering, afraid that if she cried he would strike her again. He gripped her hair even harder as her head connected with the bathroom sink and she fell to the floor.

"Get up!" he screamed.

She tried to get up, but he kicked her back down sending her crashing to the floor on her stomach. He grabbed her by the hair and drug her into the kitchen.

"Get your sorry ass up and cook Charese! I'm not going to tell you again," he warned with a threatening look on his face.

She struggled to get up.

"Oh, you don't know how to take orders?" he questioned. "But you can take dick though can't you?" he grinned.

He smacked her then made her lay on her back on the kitchen table as he got down on his knees before her. He pried her legs open and started eating her pussy like it was an all you can eat buffet. Charese didn't even enjoy it; she was emotionally drained and felt empty inside. He bit her and sucked on her clit so hard that it was far from pleasurable, then he entered her and began fucking her so hard that it caused her great pain. He swung her around like a rag doll until he got his nut, his hands around her neck the entire time. He finally loosened his grip and she sucked in as much air as possible. He jumped off her and forced his manhood down the back of her throat. He let out a loud grunt as he let his semen go into her open mouth then looked down at her and smiled.

"My baby," she whispered.

He looked at her like she disgusted him.

"Damn bitch, nobody gives a fuck about your little bastard baby." He retrieved the washcloth from the bathroom, wiped himself off, then threw it at her.

She just laid there crying. He got up and left the room. He came back fully dressed.

"Fuck it, I'll make another bitch cook," he said as he threw a stack of money at her. "I'll call you."

He left and she laid on her kitchen floor and cried.

Chapter Thirty-One

Charese's phone had been ringing nonstop for three weeks. She just couldn't answer it, not unless it was Kane, she wouldn't dare miss any of his calls. Someone had been knocking on her door on numerous occasions, but she refused to answer it. Taye, Courtni, and even a few clients yelled through the door that they knew she was home. She just couldn't face anyone. All of the pride and self-confidence that she once possessed, Kane had stripped away.

Just a week ago, he had her at a hotel under false pretenses. He told her that it was for the two of them, but when she arrived, there were a room full of studs. She had to dance for them but things took a terrible turn for the worse when Kane left her alone and let them have their way with her; she had been raped by eleven women. Her vagina was still sore. She had no appetite but she nibbled on things here and there. More for her son than herself.

Kane found a family to take her son who agreed to sign legal documents stating that they would surrender all rights once Charese was ready to take care of him. She did want to be a mother; she just wasn't ready to be one now. She had a good chunk of change already saved up, but she needed more. She had things to do. She had to finish school, get her son back, and create a new life for herself in the process.

One Month Later

"That's it Miss Shaw, you're doing wonderful," the doctor said as she continued to push. The pain was unbearable, causing her to scream as she pushed again. Push. Scream. Push. Scream. Push! Charese heard her baby cry; he had a nice set of lungs. She smiled and fell back on a pillow as the nurse wiped her head.

She was alone. She called Tee while she was caged up in her apartment and told him her situation. He wanted her back until she broke the news of her pregnancy and that he was possibly the father. He denied her son, hung up on her, then promptly changed his phone number. She ran into him about a week ago and begged him to take a paternity test, but he refused. She still was unsure of who the father was which was all the more reason why she felt like she was doing the right thing for her son by giving him a solid foundation in a two-parent home. The Bryson's were an old Christian couple. Reynard Bryson was a pastor and his wife, Anna ran a daycare.

She looked over at her baby who was being cleaned and weighed and that sight alone instantly brought tears to her eyes. She planned on calling Mrs. Bryson as soon as she got to her designated hospital room to inform her of the baby's birth. She stared at him in awe as the nurse brought him over to her.

"He's so precious," she said with a smile as she placed him in Charese's arms. She looked at him through tears; he was beautiful. He had a head full of hair and it was the curliest hair she had ever seen. He grabbed her index finger and squeezed it tight, like he knew who she was. She held him close; he was the most amazing thing that she had ever laid eyes on. It was such a priceless moment in her life and she had no one to share it with.

Aunt Kathy was in a rehab facility and Courtni and Taye were mad at her for shutting them out. She enjoyed those first few moments with her son before they took him to the nursery. She cried, knowing that she would have to give him up. They took her to her room where she drifted off to sleep. She dreamt of her son growing up and woke up in tears because she was not in the dream. Deep down she knew she was making the right decision; this was just temporary. She was going to get her son back.

She was awakened by the doctor entering the room. He gave her the proper paperwork to complete. She had no idea having a child came with so much paperwork. She named her son Chase because he represented the only good thing that came out of her chasing her dreams. Chase Justin Shaw. Justin was the name of her deceased brother. After the doctor, left the nurse entered with her son.

"Would you like to feed him?" she asked.

Charese sat up in bed and reached for her son and nurse handed her the bottle and left.

"Hi Chase, I'm your mother. I will never abandon you son. Don't ever forget that. Mommy loves you," she said as she kissed his tiny forehead. She called the Bryson's and told them that Chase was here. Mrs. Bryson told her they would be by the next day to visit her and the baby.

That following afternoon she introduced Chase to his new family and cried. Mrs. Bryson hugged her tightly, promising her that she could visit Chase any time she wanted to. They stayed for a while then told her that they would be back once she was discharged, so she could have as much alone time with her son as possible.

The day she came home from the hospital, she was an emotional wreck. The hardest thing she ever had to do was watch the Bryson's leave with her child. She kissed him a million times before she handed him over and promised him that they would be together as a family one day and she meant it. Mrs. Bryson encouraged her to come by and see him any time she felt like it. She wanted Chase to be familiar with her so he wouldn't feel like he was leaving with a stranger whenever she was ready to come take him for good.

She was home blasting Big Sean's latest mix tape through her speakers while lying across her living room floor drinking Chardonnay straight from the bottle. She looked at the pictures of her son and started crying. That's all she had been doing since her hospital release; crying. She couldn't help but wonder what he was doing and how he was being treated. She had a good feeling about the Bryson's so she quickly blocked out any negative thoughts. She knew in her heart that her son was ok.

She got up and changed from the CD player to "The Quiet Storm" on the radio, turned off all her lights and laid on the couch and wished that she could change her life.

Chapter Thirty-Two

It was March and Charese's twenty-third birthday was coming up. She just stopped to see Chase. She came bearing toys, clothes, and four pairs of new shoes. She would sit and stare at him for hours but she couldn't see any resemblance of Tee or Bryce, he looked exactly like her. She would have to wait until he was older because she was sure that his features would change. He was happy and his eyes lit up every single time he saw her. She was very grateful for that.

So far, he was doing just fine with the Bryson's. Mrs. Bryson was her guardian angel and a better mother than she could ever be. At least right now. They all agreed that if Chase was of age to understand what was going on that they would be honest with him about the arrangement. She didn't want to lie to her son. No one from Anderson knew her son existed and she preferred it that way. She didn't need anybody in her business or judging her.

She stopped having sex with Kane for the extra money. Her son changed her point of view regarding a lot of things. Although they were no longer having sex, she was still working at the club and she had to sleep with him in order to keep all of her earnings. She had a year of school left and enough in her bank account to make ends meet.

She planned on finding a vacant building and turning it into a hair salon after she graduated which was why she continued working at the club, she still needed money. She wanted to pay cash for her shop instead of taking out one of those god-awful bank loans.

When she was stable and on her feet well enough, then and only then would she get Chase back. She was already putting in applications for a two-bedroom apartment in the Simpsonville and Greenville areas. She had also requested a transfer at her current complex. Although Gateway Village was small, it was very quiet and exactly what she needed for her son.

She was back at the club and would give head at the club for five hundred, you could fuck her for a stack, and if you had ten stacks then she would allow more than one man to fuck her at the same time. Kane, the club, and the money turned her out. Kane didn't like her "fuck fest" because he couldn't get a piece, but she didn't care. He wasn't controlling her like he used to; she was slowly, but surely getting her confidence back. Kane was beginning to get jealous so he would find any and every reason to fine her at the club. She didn't plan on staying there that much longer so nothing he did fazed her. She turned on her music and fell asleep on the couch.

When she woke up the next morning, she realized that she had overslept. She took a shower then slipped on some white jeans, a green baby tee, some green flip-flops, and pulled her hair back into a ponytail. She was glad that Chase hadn't ruined her shape as she stared at herself in the mirror. Thanks to her current membership at the gym and the extra pounds that Chase put on her, Charese's body was banging. She could give Buffy the Body a run for her money. Her waist was super thin and her once firm ass now jiggled like Jell-O. Her legs were to die for and she was okay with that.

She hopped on I-85 and headed to Anderson. Once she arrived at the club, she grabbed her bag, locked her doors, and headed straight for the locker rooms. When she opened the door two women were kissing. They didn't let her sudden entrance interrupt them and she didn't pass any judgement, seeing as how she enjoyed playing with other women herself. She briefly thought of Tip and became aroused; she missed that juicy, pretty pussy. She dismissed the thought and started getting dressed. She put on her eight-inch heels then bumped her hair. As soon as she opened the door, they were calling her to the stage.

"Moet, get your sexy ass out her and shake that fat ass girl," the DJ screamed into the microphone.

As she walked to the stage the DJ put on "She Twerkin" by Cash Out. The song was encouraging her to grind on the pole and that's exactly what she did. She took off her top as she winded her body down to the ground. She danced and collected money. When she was sure she had the crowd, she broke Kane's number one rule. She bent over with her back to her audience and took off her see through lace thongs showing the entire club her neatly shaven pussy. She was completely naked and both men and women were losing their minds lusting after Charese.

She was bad and her body looked even better. She slid her panties through the pretty slit that sat between her legs then threw her panties to the crowd and the men went wild. She blew them a kiss as the song went off and started gathering her money. Just when the crowd thought she was through, she got on all fours and started shaking her ass. She then turned around and laid on her back. The club got a good view as the watched her insert three fingers inside herself and then put her fingers in her mouth. Men ran to the stage throwing more money at her. The club was in an uproar and every nigga in the club was grabbing their crotches, including Kane. He was pissed that she was naked, but he enjoyed the show. The floor was covered with hundreds and twenties.

Some fine ass man walked up to her and put one hundred dollars in her garter belt. She grabbed his hands and put them on her ass allowing him to squeeze both her cheeks. She then climbed the pole, going all the way to the top before she spiraled down and hit the floor with a split. The men were going crazy! She waved goodnight then exited the stage. As she made her way to the locker room she was given so many compliments on the show she had just put on. Men were grabbing her and trying to get her attention left and right.

"Damn girl, I ain't know you had all that in you!" said one man.

"Where that shit come from Moet?" asked another.

"Can I lick your fingers?" she heard someone else say. The fine man from the stage grabbed her as she reached the door.

"Hey, can I get a private show?" he asked.

She smiled at him and walked into the dressing room with a couple of girls walking in after her.

"You did your thing out there girl," one stripper said.

"Thanks," she smiled again as she put her money in her bag then locked it inside her locker. She changed into a yellow thong bikini and some yellow pumps then walked back out to the club. As she walked through the club, she pushed her bikini to the top so that her breast and nipples would be exposed. A man grabbed her by the hand and held up a fifty-dollar bill, the price of a table dance. She gave him the show of his life. Afterwards, he took her to the bar and brought her a couple of drinks. She sat and talked with him for a while until she heard someone whisper in her ear.

"Let me talk to you for a minute." It was Kane.

She knew his voice without turning around. She also knew that he wasn't too pleased with her after the stunt she had just pulled.

She turned around to see that Kane was joined by four men. She really didn't want to walk with him, but said, "Um, ok," instead. She followed him as he grabbed her by the hand and led her into his office.

Chapter Thirty-Three

Charese had just gotten home to her house on Nardin Avenue. She put her money up, showered, then got dressed. Her phone beeped indicating that she had a text message. Kane screenshot his conversation with the men listing their needs for tonight and their location. She left and headed for I-85 to meet Kane and the four men he was with at the club. They had given her ten stacks to have sex with each of them and perform oral on them all. There was no way that she was passing up that kind of money. She arrived at the Hilton and retrieved her room key. When she got to the room all the men were sloppy drunk and Kane was nowhere in sight.

"Oh, there she go!" said one man as another shoved a drink in her face.

"Go ahead and drink up ma," he said.

She took the drink but didn't drink it. She stood still as another man started rubbing her ass, she suddenly felt uncomfortable.

The first man said to his friend, "Man calm down! We got plenty of time for that."

"Where's Kane?" she asked as she watched the last man get undressed.

He stripped down to his boxers. Upon refilling his drink, he walked over to Charese.

He said, "I'd like to propose a toast to the fun we're about to have tonight," never taking his eyes off Charese. The men laughed as if they were in on a joke that she knew nothing about.

"Drink it," the first man ordered.

"No thanks," she politely declined. She was getting very uncomfortable; she decided that she was going to leave. The man snatched her drink from her hand.

"Drink it!" he said as he grabbed her by the back of the head and poured the liquor down her throat.

She tried to scream, but no sound came out. He threw her on the bed. She sucked in as much air as possible, trying to catch her breath. The man grabbed her by the feet, pulling her to the end of the bed. He smacked her so hard that her lip split open.

"Yo, I got first," he told his friends. His manhood was standing at attention as he lustfully stared at the chocolate beauty lying before him. He took his pants off and put his penis in her face. She already knew what he wanted. She grabbed it and slowly put it in her mouth.

"Suck it like your life depends on it. You're one of those Fantasy thots, I know you know how to suck dick better than that!" he said as he grabbed the back of her head and forced himself down her throat, causing her to vomit.

"Damn nigga!" one of his friends said, "you're gonna kill the bitch before I get my turn!" He laughed.

Charese started crying. He stopped then entered her. He finally caught his rhythm and didn't care that he was hurting her. By that time, she couldn't control her tears. He came in her mouth then pushed her back down on the bed. She tried to get up, but another man mounted her. He grabbed her by the legs and opened them wide.

He looked down at her. "This pussy so pretty," he said as he entered her. He was beating her vagina something serious while sticking two fingers into her anus. She started crying loudly.

"Make this bitch shut up," one man said while waiting his turn. His friend started rummaging through a duffle bag then handed him a pistol and he put it against her head. The tears still fell like a waterfall, but she remained silent. His friend came inside of her then turned her around.

"Get him back right," he demanded, referring to his manhood. She began to perform oral sex on the man, but gasped when she felt someone else enter her from behind.

He had no mercy. She stopped performing oral sex for the man because it felt like his friend was ripping her apart from the inside out. The man became angry and hit her with the butt of the gun.

"GET HIM RIGHT! NOW!" he yelled. He gave his friend the gun and put both hands on the back of her head so that she couldn't move if she wanted to. His friend penetrated her ass just as he nutted on her head. She was disgusted. They finally stopped and just when she thought it was over, another one grabbed her. She cried loudly as one man penetrated her ass while the other penetrated her vagina. They had no mercy on her and she began to bleed. By the time they had all had their way with her, she was an emotional wreck.

They all stood in a circle and forced her to fellatio on all of them until they came on her. Her body reeked of dried semen, dried blood, and alcohol. Kane still had not shown up and by this time Charese had figured out that he set her up. He knew what was going to happen to her all along. She lay on the bed whimpering as the men cleaned themselves up and got dressed. The first man came over and started sucking on her nipples extremely hard. He started biting them. She put her face in a pillow to muffle her sounds. He then spread her legs and fucked her again.

She was very sore so she experienced excruciating pain. The other men started to leave.

"I'm bored with that bitch now," one said

"I got me a couple of good nuts bruh!" said another as they high-fived each other.

"We'll be in the car," the last one said to the man that was still enjoying his piece of Charese.

"Y'all go 'head" he said between grunts. "I'm getting my twenty thousand worth!"

They left the room and the man kept right on going. They had sex for an additional hour before he stopped. When her vagina dried up, he would take her ass. He handled Charese like she was nothing. When he finally finished he started getting dressed. He threw a washcloth at her.

"Clean your ass up before you walk out of here and you better not say shit girl or we're gonna kill you!" he threatened. "A nigga don't need another rape charge." He walked out the door. She ran behind him and locked the door as she shut it. She started screaming as the tears fell uncontrollably. Not only did Kane set her up but he tried to get over on her as well. He told her that they were paying ten thousand and it was all hers, but her attacker had just confirmed that he charged them double. She couldn't believe it! She cried and cried until she could cry no more. She cleaned herself up and nursed her wounds to the best of her ability then grabbed her Michael Kors sunglasses from her matching purse and left the room.

Once inside her car, she headed straight to Anderson and went home and took a bath. She put on a white wife beater with some velour pants, and her LeBrons. She applied heavy makeup to conceal her bruises then fixed her hair to cover her face and the gash that she got from the man striking her with the gun. She looked at herself and cried again. She put on her Ray Ban sunglasses because they were bigger and left her home headed straight to club Fantasy. She was not gonna let Kane get away with doing that to her. When she got there, she left her car running and her door wide open as she ran inside the club. She walked into his office without knocking but he was not there. She ran back out into the club and started screaming his name while searching for him. She found him at the bar taking inventory.

"You sorry motherfucker!" she screamed at him.

All eyes were on her as everyone stopped what they were doing to watch the drama unfold. Charese didn't care. Fresh tears rolled off her cheeks hitting her shirt like rainfall. He looked at her as if he didn't have a care in the world. A female bartender came over and put her arm around Charese.

"You okay Moet?" she asked, genuinely concerned.

Charese paid her no mind. Her eyes remained on Kane.

"Business is business," he said with a smirk. "You got your cut."

She stared at him in disbelief. "You're a fucking monster!" she screamed at the top of her lungs. Wide eyed, she grabbed a liter-sized bottle of E&J and threw it at him. He ducked as it crashed into the wall into a million tiny fragments. He looked at the shattered glass, brushed some off his shoulders, then looked at her like she was crazy. He reached for his gun, but a bouncer stopped him.

Putting his hands on top of Kane's he said, "It's a lot of witnesses in here, think about what you're doin'."

Kane kept his hands on the gun and his eyes on Charese.

Chapter Thirty-Four

He watched Charese as she stormed into the club through the front door. He never saw her come through the front door, always the back. He had heard about her little performance last night and decided to check up on her. He heard about her dancing a while ago, but he didn't believe it. He came one night and sure enough, there she was pussy poppin' on a handstand. He'd come to watch her every night after that making sure that he was never seen. She stopped talking to him over two years ago without any explanation. When he heard that she was dealing with an out of town dude and then Bryce, he was devastated. He had loved her with his whole heart and she played him.

He didn't mind spending money on her as long as he had her, but it seems that's the only time that she would deal with him, when he was spending money. He sat and watched Charese go off on Kane at the bar. Whatever it was, he knew it was serious when he witnessed her throw a liquor bottle at him. When he saw Kane reach for his gun, he decided to take action. He reached the bar just as Kane was taking his hand off his gun.

The bouncer said, "Please just leave."

The bartender agreed, "Yea, whatever it is girl, it ain't worth dying over!"

"Just let me take you home Reesy," he said.

She turned around and looked at him and facial expression went from anger to shock. She couldn't believe it! She hadn't seen him since she lived on Spencer Street.

"Mekhi?" she said in disbelief.

He put his arms around her. "You have no business being in here anyway. Let me walk you to your car," he said.

"Let him play Superman and save your life hoe!" Kane said.

She tightened her fist and took a step in his direction, but Mekhi grabbed her by the waist pulling her towards the door.

"Come on," he pleaded with her. He wasn't trying to go to war with Kane; he wasn't about that life. He took her outside.

"Hey," he started to say but she jumped in her car and sped off. Surprised, he ran to his own car and took off after her. He caught up with her about three blocks down and decided to follow her, but keep his distance. He followed her to what he assumed was her home. She was walking up the stairs as he was getting out of his car.

"I'm not leaving until you talk to me," he said opening the gate and walked up the stairs behind her. She was crying as she stared at him, keys still in the door. She looked at him.

"Come on Reesy, open up. Let me in," he said, his words having more meanings than one.

She turned the keys then opened the door, walked straight into the next room and laid on her bed, still crying. He walked in behind her, turning on the light as he came in. She stopped crying and looked at the wall. She didn't acknowledge his presence or even look his way. He walked into the kitchen, turning on the light as he entered. He searched her bare cabinets until he found some coffee; he made a pot and poured them both a cup.

"Here, drink this," he said as he sat down on the bed beside her.

She took the cup.

"Now tell me what's going on."

She remained silent, sipping on her coffee.

"Come on," he nudged her, "I'm here for you."

"Do you know how many people have told me that and left me?" she said flatly.

"You left me remember," he said.

She looked down at the floor, sighed heavily then told him everything. She started off from when she met Tee after he came to her door looking for a phone. She cut him off completely after meeting him. She admitted that she was only using him for money. She told him about Porsche, Bryce, she left out Chase, and ended with where he found her at. They talked all night and despite everything, he told her that he was still very much in love with her and wanted another chance to be with her. He wanted a real shot this time.

She did have money saved up, and she was about to graduate, but she still didn't have enough money for her shop. The ten thousand she earned tonight now seemed worthless to her. If she and Mekhi started talking again, she knew he would give her money any time she asked for it. She could use his money for her shop and keep her money in her pocket but that attitude contributed to her current situation. Money was the reason she was going through so much, money was the common denominator in all of her problems. She couldn't keep her son like she wanted to or live the life she wanted to. Why? Money, she exhaled deeply. She was emotionally drained.

"It's okay," he said consoling her.

She started crying again. When she finally stopped crying they both sat in silence. The only sounds heard were her quiet whimpers. He jerked her up in his arms and hugged her tight then just held her. He held her until she cried herself to sleep.

Chapter Thirty-Five

ONE YEAR LATER

Charese was on her way to pick up Chase for some ice cream. It was her twenty-fourth birthday, and who better to celebrate with than her son. This birthday would definitely be better than last year when she was gang raped; some party that turned out to be. Chase had just turned one in January. He looked exactly like her so she still had a hard time figuring out who his father was. Bryce was still not around and Tee was still acting like a jackass. If she could just find Bryce and get him to take a paternity test then it would make things a lot easier for her.

If he was the father then she knew he would be in Chase's life, and if not, then she would know for sure that Tee was the father and she could slap him with child support. That's all she wanted from Tee, support and nothing more. She pulled up at the Bryson's to see Chase's cocoa brown face smiling in the window. She got out the car just as Mrs. Bryson was helping him down the stairs.

"Mommy," he screamed with delight.

She bent over and scooped him up in her arms planting a million kisses on his face causing him to squeal. She ran her hands through his hair, which was curlier than the day he was born.

"Hey baby!" she said as she hugged him tight.

"Hello Charese," Mrs. Bryson said as she was putting Chase down.

Charese said hello as they hugged each other.

"So where are you guys headed?" Mrs. Bryson asked.

"Well, today is my birthday."

"Happy birthday," Mrs. Bryson said interrupting her.

"So we're going to Bruster's for ice cream," she finished.

"Yay!" said Chase.

She got his car seat out of her trunk and buckled him up in the car.

"We'll be back in the next two hours or so," Charese said.

"Okay," she said she waved goodbye to Chase.

"Bye Mama Ann," he said to her calling her by his name for her.

They left and headed to Bruster's. Once they got there, she ordered a vanilla cone for Chase and a large banana split for herself. He devoured his then helped Charese eat hers. Her phone rang it was Mekhi.

"Hey baby," she cooed as she answered.

"What's up? Where you at?" he asked.

"Um, out in Greenville," she said.

"What's in Greenville?" he wanted to know.

"I'm visiting my grandmother," she lied.

"Oh okay, what time you getting home?" he asked.

"Soon," was her reply.

"Well okay ... miss you," he said

"I miss you too," she said with a smile.

"Mommy look!" Chase yelled while holding a cherry stem on his nose.

"Who was that?" he asked.

"Um, my little cousin. Let me call you back," she said as she hung up on him.

"Mommy," Chase said again.

"Yes baby?" she answered sweetly. She loved her son dearly.

"Pee pee," he said while holding himself.

She rushed him to the restroom. The Bryson's were doing a wonderful job with him. He was very advanced for a child that only had one year under his belt. Her phone rang again and it was Mekhi. She answered.

"What's your problem?" he barked into the phone.

"Nothing baby. I'm sorry," she apologized.

"Okay," he said as he softened his tone.

"I love you," she said.

"I love you too," he replied affectionately.

"I'll be home soon," she said.

They ended their call. She didn't know how much longer she would be able to keep Chase a secret especially since she and Mekhi were getting serious about each other. She gave up both her places and moved in with him. She looked at Chase. He was getting bigger by the minute and eventually, she was going to want him back. She was graduating next week and Mekhi was going to help her get her shop off the ground. Charese found out that he had done a lot with himself after their first fling ended; he was an architect.

He was in school back when they were talking so she knew he would amount to something. She got him to re-enroll in school so now he was going for business management. She planned on getting Chase back once her shop was up and running, but she would also have to have a very long and serious talk with Mekhi before she took that step. That's when she would tell him about her son.

She and Chase ended up at the movies before she took him home. By the time she returned him to the Bryson's, he was sound asleep. She grabbed him, the bag of toys she had purchased, and walked up the stairs. Mrs. Bryson opened the door and let them in. She kissed her son on the forehead then again on his chubby cheeks before handing him to Mr. Bryson, who took him up to his room. Mrs. Bryson was sitting at the kitchen table with a book in her hand. She was reading the latest Cole Hart signature novel and was deeply engulfed in it, as usual.

"Well, I'll call later in the week!" she yelled as she headed for the door.

"Ah, Charese, can we have a minute of your time?"

"Yea, sure," she said as she took a seat at the kitchen table.

Chapter Thirty-Six

Mrs. Bryson marked her place in her book before sitting in front of her. She looked at Charese and smiled. They listened as Mr. Bryson closed Chase's bedroom door and descended the stairs. Mrs. Bryson waited for him to join them before she spoke. She grabbed Charese by the hands.

"We want to talk about Chase," she said slowly. Charese looked from her, to her husband, then back to her.

"Well, what about him?" she asked defensively.

"Well, we see that things are going in the right direction for you and that's good, we're happy for you. Now don't get me wrong, Chase is welcomed here as long as we have breath in our bodies. We are prepared to keep him forever if need be."

Charese interrupted her, "Where are you going with this?"

"We had two children, Helena and Rich. Both died some years ago in a terrible car accident along with my niece. We tried to have another child for years but were unsuccessful so we just gave up. We went to numerous doctors and different specialists and we still couldn't figure out why we weren't able to conceive. I became depressed and didn't want to try anymore. That was fifteen years ago, she paused as she grabbed a Kleenex.

She continued, "So anyway, Reynard came home with a brochure from a foster care facility. I never once even entertained that idea; I wanted a child of my own. Reynard would drag me from one house to the next. Although we came across some cute children, I just didn't feel anything for any of them. So when Keenan came to us about your child I was kind of skeptical."

Charese cut her off, "Keenan?" she questioned.

Mrs. Bryson looked at her clearly confused. "Yes, Keenan sweetie, my nephew that you were dealing with."

"Who Kane?" Charese asked, surprised.

"Kane Mercy, the names you kids today come up with these days, but if that's what he calls himself then okay," she said with a chuckle. She shook her head then continued on with her story.

"But the Christian in me just couldn't look the other way once he told me your story. I knew I had to take that child. So he told me you were still with child and I grew excited. I was getting a newborn baby to start fresh with. But I will admit; I was extremely upset when I was told that you would eventually want him back. What I'm getting at, Charese, we know the time is coming and you're going to want to take Chase home soon. I don't want him to go."

Charese started to protest, but Mrs. Bryson held up her hand to quiet her.

"But I know that child needs his mother and I know you need your son. I know you were in a bad situation. I don't know all the details, but I know enough. You were with my nephew so I can only imagine."

Mr. Bryson took over. "When that day comes we want you to talk to us first. Don't just take him away from us. We want it to be a smooth transition for Chase, but we also want to spend time alone with him. We love Chase deeply," he said full of emotion.

Mrs. Bryson grabbed her hands and looked her in the eyes through fresh tears.

"And please don't keep him away from us baby. We would love to still be a part of his life," she pleaded.

"Of course," Charese said as she squeezed her hand.

"Anna and I have been talking about this for quite some time and we were hoping that we all could get papers drawn up through our lawyers."

"What kind of papers?" Charese asked getting defensive again.

"Hear me out... the papers would simply state that in your absence we would like to act as legal guardians."

Charese exhaled a sigh of relief as she put her hand over her chest. "Whew! I thought you guys were going to say you were trying to fight me for custody or something," she said.

"Heavens no!" they said in unison and both laughed.

"Well, that's fine with me. Who better to have him than you guys anyway?"

Mrs. Bryson leaped from her chair with joy. Charese laughed aloud.

"You guys know that my parents are both dead and gone right? So maybe you guys could act as their stand-ins," she suggested.

Mrs. Bryson got up and walked around to Charese's side of the table.

She hugged her tight. "Of course," she said.

Mr. Bryson smiled and got up to hug her as well and they walked her to the front door.

"I'll call later in the week," she said to them. She got into her car and then headed home. Mekhi's house was in a good neighborhood. They lived in a four-bedroom, two and a half bathroom house in the Concord area. She got home in record time and as soon as she walked in Mekhi was sitting on the couch in the dark waiting on her.

"I was wondering when you were going to come home," he said.

"Damn baby, I'm sorry. I just lost track of time," she apologized.

He stood before her and looked her in the eyes.

Grabbing her by the shoulders he said, "I want you to be honest with me Reesy."

"Um, okay," she said, afraid of what he was about to ask her.

"Are you cheating on me?" he wanted to know.

"Oh my gosh! No Mekhi! No baby, now come on, you've been nothing but good to me. Why would I hurt you?" she assured him as she kissed him passionately on the lips. His lips left hers as they traveled, until his mouth found their way to her hardened nipple. He tugged at it gently before picking her up and carrying her to the bedroom.

Chapter Thirty-Seven

"I'm so happy for you baby!" Mekhi said for the one hundredth time.

They were at Golden Corral celebrating her graduation. She was now a licensed cosmetologist who had a degree in business management. "The only thing left to do now is find a place for your shop."

She looked at him a squealed and put her arms around his neck, planting a million kisses on his cheek. "Oh thank you baby! I love you! I love you! I love you!" she exclaimed while crying tears of joy.

He kissed her tears before wiping her face. "My lady deserves the best and I'm going to do everything in my power to make sure you have that," he assured her.

She smiled. "Well baby," she hesitated, "I need to discuss something very important with you." She decided that now was the right time to tell him about Chase.

"What is it?" he asked.

"Well um, I don't know where to start," she started crying and he came over and sat beside her.

"Talk to me baby, what's wrong?" he coaxed.

She had never been more afraid of anything in her life than she was right now. She was afraid that he would be mad at her, afraid that he wouldn't accept Chase, afraid that he wouldn't love her anymore.

"There's not an easy way to say this," she started. "Well, there is another man in my life," she looked down at the ground.

Before she could say anything else, he jerked his hands away from hers and began to get loud.

"What the fuck are you talking about Charese?" he yelled as everyone's attention turned to them.

"Baby, hold on. Let me explain," she pleaded as he stood up.

"What is there to explain Charese? I gave you everything!" he said clearly heartbroken.

By now, the entire restaurant was silent as all eyes were on them.

"Baby please, wait," she ran behind him as he headed for the nearest exit. She caught up to him and grabbed him by his shirt. He pushed her off him so hard that she fell on the ground.

"Stay the fuck away from me Charese!" he warned.

A waitress helped her off the ground and she took off after him, running into a couple on her way out. The Bryson's, and they had Chase with them. She cried as she explained to them what was going on and asked if she could take Chase with her and agreed. After getting his car seat from its' hiding place in her trunk, she grabbed her son and took off after her boyfriend.

Once she arrived home, she was relieved that Mekhi was there. She parked her car and took her son out of the backseat. When she walked inside, she couldn't believe her eyes. He trashed the entire living room. She went upstairs and walked into their bedroom and Mekhi was throwing all of her belongings into suitcases. He stopped when she walked into the room.

"Come pack the rest of your shit!" he said.

"Mekhi," she said, hoping that he would calm down but he just continued to pack her clothes.

"Mekhi," she repeated.

"Whose baby is that?" he asked without looking up.

She hesitated before she answered. "Mine," she said barely above a whisper.

He looked at her in shock.

"This is the other man in my life. Mekhi, I want you to meet Chase, my son."

He looked from her to Chase then back to her. He stood still, dumbfounded for a minute. After coming out of his initial shock, he had a lot of questions, which she answered truthfully. He kept kissing her and apologizing for not trusting her. He kept playing with Chase and she had to admit that it felt really good watching him interact with her son. After she explained everything, he asked her why she kept it a secret. He interrupted her in mid-sentence when he was suddenly hit with the idea to go shopping. He had many things he wanted to do for Chase now that he knew she existed. Charese was overjoyed.

Chapter Thirty-Eight

It had been a couple of weeks since she first introduced Mekhi to Chase. That night he accompanied her when she took Chase back to the Bryson's. After the introductions were made, they all sat at the table and talked about Chase for hours. Charese finally decided that she was ready for him to come.

She was just leaving downtown where she had signed all the necessary paperwork to be able to bring him home. She also had the papers drawn up stating that the Bryson's were his legal guardians in her absence. She would still have to wait a couple of weeks before she would be able to bring Chase home, but that was fine with her since she had already promised them that they could have their private time with him.

Mekhi had gone completely insane; he went shopping for Chase every day. He had completely redone one of the guestrooms into a room for Chase by painting the walls blue and giving his room a sports theme. He handmade Chase a basketball shaped bed with a wooden net as the headboard. The bed looked as if someone had just made a shot. It was so cute and huge; Chase would be able to use it for years if he wanted to. He even had a basketball goal built in from his wall and a million toys, clothes, and shoes.

Charese was so happy. She had been spending her time kid proofing the house, taking extra precautions to make sure that Chase didn't get hurt. She was a bit nervous because never had her son full time. Being a real mommy was about to be a first for her. It would take some getting used to, but she was sure that her family would be fine. She was mopping the kitchen floor when her phone rang.

"Hello," she said as she answered it.

"Where are you?" It was Mekhi.

"At home cleaning," she answered.

"Get dressed. I'm about to come get you," he said. She got dressed and waited for Mekhi to pull up.

"What's up baby?" she asked as she got in the car.

"You'll see," he said as he blindfolded her.

She tried to protest, but he wouldn't let her take it off. Once she felt the car stop, she asked,

"Where are we?"

He got out and opened her door. "Get out," he said as he grabbed her by the hand.

"What's going on?" she asked.

"You know I love you right?" he said.

"Yes, and I love you too," said a blindfolded Charese.

"I want you to have everything you ever wanted. I want to give you the world."

"Aww baby, that's so sweet," she said as she smiled.

He took the blindfold off and she felt someone tap her shoulder. She was surprised to turn around and see Courtni standing behind her. She started screaming and crying at the same time.

"Oh my gosh! Girl, I've missed you so much!" Charese said through tears.

"I've missed you too." She, too, had started crying.

She playfully smacked Mekhi on the arm. "How'd you pull this off baby?" she asked.

"Ran into her," he said and shrugged his shoulders.

"But how? Where?" she wanted to know. She was so happy, she hugged Courtni again.

"Yep, and he gave me the 411 on you girl," Courtni teased.

"Oh really?" Charese said with her hands on her hips.

"Yes really," she said. "He told me that I could come get these naps done too."

"Yea girl, of course. Just follow us home," Charese said still beaming. She was genuinely happy to see her best friend.

"So you're gonna make me go to your house instead of just doing it here?"

"What?" asked a confused Charese. "Don't you want your hair done?"

"Yes, but I was hoping to be the first one in your chair. Plus, I want to check out the inside!" Courtni said excitedly.

"Now how in the hell am I supposed to do your hair outside?" Charese laughed while stating the obvious.

Courtni smiled, "Oh yea, I forgot you aren't even open yet."

"Huh?" she asked.

Mekhi cleared his throat, getting Charese's attention. He reached into his pockets then dangled some keys in front of her.

"Well, she's open now," he said with a smile and placed the keys in her hand. She stood there, not yet registering what was going on. .

"Open the door girl before people see me with my hair looking like this," Courtni urged.

Charese was stunned in place. Then she looked at the white building standing before her that she hadn't noticed before.

"Baby, no you didn't!" she screamed.

"Yes I did," he confirmed.

She jumped up and down screaming and hugging his neck the entire time. She started crying again she was so happy. She ran to the door and opened it. When she walked in, she couldn't believe her eyes. The place was already fully furnished. She noticed a lot of the things were things she had circled in a catalog months ago. She had no idea that he had been paying attention.

"You told me you were looking for a place to house your architectural firm," she scolded.

"I lied," he admitted.

"It's beautiful baby," she said and meant it. She was already in love with the place. The place was done in Cherry wood and looked very professional and neat. She had a lobby, and space for a nail tech and a barber if she wanted one. He already had all the hair products and supplies; he had set her up nicely. She had hardwood floors and floor-to-ceiling mirrors on the wall. The place was exactly how she dreamt her shop would be.

"And how did you know that I would like this?" she asked Mekhi.

"He may have helped a little bit," Courtni admitted.

Charese smiled as she ran her fingers across the marble countertops. She walked down the hall towards the back of the salon and entered the ladies' room and to say that it was immaculate would be an understatement. It looked like it was in a five star hotel instead of a hair salon. There were four stalls, four sinks, an area full of hair products, a changing table, a tampon dispenser and even a sitting area surrounded by Sister to Sister, Jet, and XXX magazines. She fought back tears as she walked over to the men's room; it was plain.

"You know men don't live in the bathroom like y'all," he joked.

They all laughed. She went to the end of the hall and opened the last door, only to see everything that she picked out for her future office. Charese was beside herself. She was truly speechless. There was a full-length fish tank with a myriad of animals inhabiting it. She even had a two way mirror in front of her desk so that she could see her employees, but her they couldn't see her. Anyone that knew her knew that she loved mirrors and candles and her shop was full of both. She sat at her desk and cried some more, she had never been this happy in her life.

"Aww, go 'head with all that Reesy, you're supposed to be happy," Courtni said, admiring the salon.

She ran over to Mekhi and kissed him again. "Thank you so much baby! I love you!" she cooed.

"I love you too."

They continued kissing and Courtni left them in the shop as she checked out the rest of the building. When they left the office, they found her swirling in one of the chairs at one of the booths.

"I think I like this station right here. It's right by the lounge and I like to eat," she said with a laugh.

"Lounge?" Charese asked.

Courtni pointed to a door that read "Employees Only" and followed Charese as she walked in. There had a large sectional surrounding a coffee table that sat right in front of a plasma TV that mounted the wall. She counted four plasma TV's out on the floor; Mekhi had outdone himself. There was a full kitchen area fully equipped with any and every appliance you could possibly need. In the back of the room were a set of lockers, which she assumed would belong to her employees. Next to the locker was a storage closet and Mekhi already had it well stocked, her shop was all set and she didn't have to lift a finger.

Chapter Thirty-Nine

SIX MONTHS LATER

Today was the day that she was bringing Chase home. The timing couldn't have been better because it was right before Christmas. Their tree was already up and Chase already had a million presents under it. Everyone had been talking to Chase about what was about to happen, but still, no one knew what to expect. Charese was shitting bricks she was so nervous. Chase had been staying over every weekend, but she still didn't know how he would adjust to the change.

She was leaving her shop after interviewing potential employees. She still had not opened her shop to the public yet, she wanted everything to be perfect. She was looking for four more stylists; of course she had already hired Courtni. She also hired two nail techs, two receptionist, and two janitors. She had been holding open interviews every day from two to four. She planned on conducting these interviews for the next two weeks. After that, she would choose candidates that would come back for a second interview. If they did well on the second interview then she would have them work on a mannequin's head in front of her. Whichever ones impressed her the most would get the spots.

This last girl, Peaches, was not getting a call back. She had ratchet and ghetto written all over her and Charese was not having that in her place of business. She locked her doors just as Mekhi was pulling up.

"Hey baby. You okay?" he asked sincerely.

"Just nervous," she said as they hugged.

They got into the car and headed to the Bryson's. The ride over was silent as each of them entertained their own thoughts. Both thinking of how things would change once Chase was around permanently. He had a room and a playroom so she was sure that he wouldn't have a problem adjusting. They were both hoping for a smooth transition. When they arrived Chase was playing in the front yard while the Bryson's were sitting on the front porch watching him. When they pulled in the old couple got up and met them in the yard.

They all talked and made an agreement that Chase would stay with them every other weekend and that he would still come to Mrs. Bryson every day after Head Start. Mrs. Bryson began to cry when it was time for Chase to leave. Chase ran over to them and hugged them both tightly.

Mr. Bryson played in his curly hair. "We're going to miss you around here kiddo," he smiled through his own tears.

Mrs. Bryson spoke, "You're about to go live with your mommy now okay?

"Okay," he said.

"I'm going to miss you baby," she said as she started crying all over again.

"Okay," he repeated.

She laughed then looked at Charese.

"He's all yours," she sighed heavily.

They hugged each other, now it was Charese's turn to cry.

"Thank you, for everything," she said.

Mrs. Bryson nodded her head in acknowledgement and they hugged again. They hugged and kissed Chase once before Charese picked him up and put him in the car. Mekhi loaded all of his belongings into the trunk then they headed home.

Chase and Mekhi bonded instantly once they brought him home. After two weeks, Chase walked around the house as if he owned it.

She was at the shop and had just held her final interviews. She had six stylists: Courtni, Diamond, Tab,

Kiki, Liz, and Domonique. They each had something unique to bring to her shop. Courtni and Tab were master barbers like herself so they could do anything. Diamond specialized in extensions and tracks and was nineteen, Kiki specialized in twist and dreads and was twenty-one, Liz was thirty-two and specialized in natural hair, and Domonique was considered the braid queen at only twenty years old. She started making the calls to the women to let them know that they had all been hired. She had already hired Nikki and Anoki as her nail technicians and two men named Kentrell and Marcus as her barbers.

She informed them all that orientation and a meet and greet was scheduled for the following Monday then locked up and headed home. When she got there, Chase and Mekhi were heading out. They both hugged and kissed her as she reached the door.

"I was about to take him to the Bryson's," he told her.

"Okay baby," she said. She looked at Chase and gave him a big kiss on the cheek and said, "I will see you Sunday little man."

He giggled. She watched them pull off then went inside and locked the door. As soon as she walked into her bedroom her cell phone rang, it was Courtni.

"What's up boo?" Charese asked when she answered.

"Nothing darling, just being fabulous!" she stated as they shared a laugh.

"Girl what do you want? I'm about to take a shower," Charese said.

"Come outside."

"Huh?" She looked out the window in time to see Courtni pulling into her driveway. She walked outside just as Courtni and Taye were getting out of the car.

"Taye!" Charese screamed as she ran to her friend. They embraced and neither could stop the waterworks if they tried.

Chapter Forty

Taye, Courtni, and Charese were all sitting on the floor in Charese's den on the bearskin rug that she and Mekhi had made love on numerous occasions. They were all drunk; they were on their third bottle of wine. They switched to wine after drinking five apple martinis' apiece; they raided Mekhi's bar. When they heard him come in, they started giggling for no reason. Charese stood up to greet him, but her legs gave out and she fell crashing to the floor, and all three women laughed aloud. Her smile quickly faded when Mekhi entered the room; she could tell that something happened.

"What is it baby?" she asked.

"Kane is dead," he said.

Those words made Charese sober up quickly. It took her a moment to process what he had just told her. He showed her a message. Sparkle texted a friend, devastated, who in turn screenshot the entire message and forwarded it. It ended up getting to Mekhi.

"Good," was all she said as she headed to the bar and fixed herself a glass of Bacardi 151.

Mekhi took it from her before she could even take a sip.

"That's enough Reesy," he said then acknowledged her friends.

"Hi ladies," he said.

They both spoke to him.

"Well, we'll see you later Reesy," they said.

"Call me," Courtni said on their way out.

It turned out that Kane had robbed the wrong people this time. Apparently, he had pissed some men off from Augusta. Mekhi informed her that he'd questioned the Bryson's about it and from what they told him, it involved a new strip club and some missing money. On his way back to South Carolina, the men chased him down and ran him off the road. His car went down an embankment before it crashed and burned.

Charese knew it was wrong, but she was happy that he was dead. In her eyes it was long overdue. For a split second, she thought about the club and what would become of it. But that was only for a split second; she had moved on.

Charese spent the next day sleeping it away; she had a hangover from hell. She didn't eat or anything until Mekhi woke her up with breakfast in; it was Christmas Day. They ate breakfast together then made love before opening their gifts. Charese took a shower while Mekhi prepared for Chase and the Bryson's.

When she came downstairs fully dressed Mekhi was recording Chase opening his presents. She began to cry. This was the first Christmas spent with her son at their home and she was content. Chase didn't know what to do with the mountain of toys that he received. He was happy and bounced around from one corner to the other. Mr. and Mrs. Bryson sat on the couch enjoying the scene before them as well. If Chase was happy then they were happy.

Charese was so grateful for them and her many blessings. As she looked at her son, her house, and her charming boyfriend, she knew she was blessed. Her life was finally becoming worth living. After the gifts were all opened, they sat down for breakfast. She had prepared bacon, eggs benedict, salmon croquettes, French toast, pancakes, sausage, grits, and country ham.

"This all looks so wonderful Charese," Mrs. Bryson complimented after grace was said.

"Thank you," she said with a smile.

They all enjoyed their meal as different conversations took place around the table.

"Are you cooking dinner?" Mrs. Bryson asked

"Yes ma'am. You guys are more than welcomed to stay," Charese offered.

"No thanks dear, we always travel to Sylva, North Carolina to visit family until New Years," she said.

They all finished eating then said their goodbyes.

"We'll call when we return," Mr. Bryson said as they pulled off. She waved goodbye then walked back inside, locking the door behind her. Mekhi was rubbing his stomach.

"Breakfast was slamming babe," he said as he kissed her neck. They kissed but were interrupted when Chase came running into the foyer and jumped into Mekhi's arms. Charese watched with love as they wrestled with one another.

After they cleaned the house, they all left to visit some of Jon Jon's family and friends. It was twelve am when they finally returned home. They put Chase to bed before taking a shower together and heading to bed themselves.

******

Charese was undeniably happy. New Year's Day had rolled around with the grand opening of her shop and it was doing well. She had a lot of clientele and she loved her employees. Her shop was the talk of the town and things were finally looking up for her. Chase's birthday was right around the corner and they planned on throwing him a party at Cici's Pizza.

She was in her office going over her books when she heard a knock at the door. It was Mrs. Mable, one of her janitors.

"The shop has closed. Would you like me to get started?" she asked.

Charese looked at the clock, it was a little after nine pm. Where did the time go?

"Yes ma'am and when you're done you can come get your check," she said.

Mrs. Mable said okay then shut the door behind her. Just as she shut the door, her cell phone rang. She smiled as Mekhi's picture flashed across the screen.

"Hey baby," she answered with a big smile on her face.

"Come out here to your station. I have a surprise for you," was all he said.

"What?" she asked.

"Come on babe, don't make me beg," he whined.

"Alright, I'm coming," she said as she played along. She hung up and left her office.

Much to her surprise the salon was still full. In her chair sat Mekhi. Courtni was holding Chase and next to her stood Taye and her boys. Surrounding them were her employees and people that were close to her and Mekhi.

"What's all this?" she asked, directing her question at Mekhi. Mrs. Mable was standing by the door smiling from ear to ear. Charese wondered what all of this was about.

Mekhi grabbed her by the hand and sat her down in her chair. He handed her a bouquet of flowers, which she graciously accepted.

"Reesy, I have loved you even when you wouldn't give me the time of day. You are my heart's joy and the reason why it still beats. Every moment that I live is for you and Chase. Nothing would make me happier than making our family complete," he paused.

Charese held her breath.

"Charese Nicole Shaw, will you do me the honor or becoming my wife?" he asked as he pulled out the biggest diamond she had ever saw in her entire life.

The ten carats were flawless as she admired the ring. She stared at it without saying a word; she was shocked and rendered speechless all at the same time. Courtni broke her out of her daze.

"Damn bitch, say yes before I do!" she said causing everyone to laugh.

"Yes!" she exclaimed as Mekhi scooped her up from the chair and into his arms. They were surrounded by screaming and applause.

He looked into her eyes. "You're really gonna marry me?" he asked.

"Yes," she repeated.

They shared a deep, passionate kiss as all of their friends and family looked on.

Chapter Forty-One

Charese spent the next few months in complete bliss. It was the middle of April and Charese was doing something that she never thought she would do. She was planning her wedding. She just knew that her life would end tragically like everyone else she loved, but Mekhi had given her an outlet. Her Aunt passed back in February after succumbing to a stroke. She was the last living person in her immediate family. The only family she had that she knew of was her cousins Remy and Sydney, but she barely talked to them. They were at Aunt Kathy's funeral though.

One of the men that raped her in the hotel room on her birthday was even at the funeral. They recognized each other and being guilt ridden, he couldn't even face her. She went into a deep depression after that. She didn't work much and was barely planning her wedding. Mekhi was spending more time with Chase than she was. She knew that she was going to have to snap out of her pity party. Eventually, she knew that she was going to have to come around which was why she had taken two appointments that day.

She had just finished the first one when her phone rang. It was the Head Start informing her that Chase's father wanted to be added to the list of emergency contacts and people that could sign him out of school. She told them that it was fine. She really admired how Mekhi was stepping up when it came to Chase. She texted him "I love you," and he replied with "I love you more".

She left the shop and rode past the vacant building that used to be Club Fantasy, the place that housed all of her demons. She suddenly felt a cold chill that made her shiver with fear. She would have never thought that her life would come crashing down around her, that everything would fall apart right before her very eyes. Hell, she was what most niggas would call a bad bitch. She made sure that all of her shit was official and well put together. She was one of the most popular dancers at Club Fantasy.

She was Charese, or Reesy, to her friends and family, but known as Moet by the club patrons. She was bad for real though, at least in her eyes. You couldn't tell her shit, shit was beautiful and knew it. She stood at 5'5, she was one hundred and forty five pounds, thick thighs, perky 34C cups, long, jet-black hair, a fat ass, and blemish free mocha chocolate skin. She shouldn't have even been at the club, but everyone falls on hard times. She was trying to get her money right and live her dreams. Her dream was to own her own hair salon.

She ended up reaching her goal; she just wished she didn't have to go through the things she went through to get there. She was currently on her way to pick up her son Chase from school and take him to the babysitter. She was already running behind because she had a four thirty appointment. She was at a red light when she turned and locked eyes with Bryce. Bryce Westland, the man that used to make her pussy tingle and her panties wet on sight. She looked away and thanked God the light turned green. She thought back to when they used to kick it, way before shit changed.

She didn't even realize that she was speeding until she took her foot off the gas. She was sweating profusely. Where in the hell did he come from?

She pulled up at the Head Start and picked Chase up then walked him nervously back to the car. She buckled him in then got in herself. As she turned the ignition her phone rang startling her, she dropped it. As she reached down to pick it up she heard someone knock on her window. Thinking that she forgot something of Chase's, she expected to see a teacher at her door but was taken aback when her eyes met Bryce's. She froze.

"Bryce," she whispered as his name barely escaped her lips.

"Let your window down Reesy," he ordered and she obeyed.

Chapter Forty-Two

"So is he mine?" he asked.

Charese finally found her voice. "Well look who suddenly arose from the dead," she said sarcastically.

"You look good," he said as he sized her up, noticing the weight she had put on.

She stared at him. He still looked good, but had cut his hair. She noticed that he was staring at her hand, which was resting on the steering wheel.

"You married?" he asked as he looked in her the eyes.

"Engaged," she corrected him and lowered her head. The tension between them grew thick.

He broke the silence by turning his attention to Chase.

"What's up little man?" he said as Chase smiled. "Cute kid," he complimented.

"Thank you," was all she said.

"I always knew that we'd make a beautiful baby," he said confidently.

"Who said he was yours?" she asked.

"Well is he?" he countered. She remained silent.

Finally she said, "I don't know."

"Why is that Charese?" he asked.

By then she had grown frustrated and she snapped. "Why the fuck does it matter to you Bryce? Didn't you fucking abandon me? It took Kane to die for you to come back, really?" She was pissed, but there it was. She said it. There was an awkward silence between them. Any confidence that he had was gone.

"I'm sorry," he said as he looked at the ground. She turned away from him as she wiped the tears away that were threatening to fall down her face.

"I never meant to hurt you Reesy, you have to believe that. That shit with Kane and everything else I was going through was just too much on my plate. I've never been a killer and it changed me. I just had to get away. There was a lot of stuff... stuff that I was involved in that you knew nothing about. I was planning on coming back for you, I swear! Shit just didn't pan out like it was supposed to," he stared into her eyes.

She lost the battle with her tears and was wailing before she knew it. She still loved this man. Poor Chase started crying too, just from seeing his mother upset.

"But I'm here now Reesy. I wanna fix things and make it right between us," he assured her. "I was afraid for my life," he confessed.

She cut him off.

"And you didn't give a fuck about mine," she yelled.

He said nothing. She put her car in drive.

"Reesy," he said.

She ignored him. He repeated her name only louder this time.

"It wasn't like that!" he yelled as she sped off. She was a nervous wreck and in no mood to do any hair. She called and had Courtni take care of her appointment for her; she dropped Chase off at the Bryson's, then headed home where she slept.

She had been sulking in bed for two weeks. She eventually told Mekhi about what happened with Bryce. Much to her surprise, he was very understanding and supportive. It reminded her of why she was marrying him. That man really loved her. He suggested that they push the wedding date up. She knew it was because Bryce had resurfaced. She assured him that he had nothing to worry about, but he wasn't trying to hear it. They were set to marry the following week.

"You're going to have to come out of that little funk you're in," he had told her on many occasions.

She went back to the shop the next day and actually had a good day. She had just closed the shop and was outside locking up when she, Courtni, and Anoki were blinded by headlights. It was Bryce.

"Oh my gosh!" Courtni gasped. She was visibly as shocked as Anoki was confused.

"Y'all alright?" she asked.

"Yes," Charese replied without taking her eyes off of Bryce who was getting out of the car.

"Alright then, see you guys tomorrow," she said as she got in her car and left. Courtni remained by Charese's side.

"Damn, am I too late for a haircut?" he asked. "Hey there Courtni."

She was still speechless, but she waved at him.

"Damn, you're still fine as hell," he said as he put his arms around Charese. She pushed him off.

"What's wrong? You scared Mekhi might see us?" he joked.

"How did you," she started to say.

"I've done my homework Reesy," he said as he interrupted her.

"Uh, I need to get home. Reesy you straight?" Courtni asked.

"Yea, I'm right behind you," she said with her eyes still on Bryce.

"Okay, I'll call you later," she said as she got into her car and left.

"So is he my son Reesy?"

"I'm not sure. Maybe," she answered honestly.

"Well, I'd like a blood test," he stated matter-of-factly. "If he's mine I wanna be a part of his life and yours too."

"That won't be necessary," she hissed.

"Why not?" he asked.

"Mekhi takes very good care of us and I don't have to worry about him abandoning us. He really loves me."

"But you'll never love him the way that you love me!" Bryce boasted. "You still love me, don't you Reesy?"

She said nothing.

"Yes you do and to be real, we don't even need a blood test. I know that boy belongs to me," he said.

"And how do you know that?" she asked.

He pulled out some papers. They were from a DNA lab.

"How in the hell did you do this?" she yelled demanding answers.

"I simply picked my son up from school and had him tested. You said I could be added on the list remember," he stated nonchalantly.

She froze. "I thought that was Mekhi; that was you?" she asked.

"It was me," he confirmed.

She kicked herself after she remembered that Mekhi was already on the list. She obviously hadn't been thinking clearly.

"Oh my gosh," she said more to herself than to Bryce.

"Oh my gosh is right," he mocked her. "I want to see my son Charese."

"You had no right to do that!" she screamed. She was crying now.

"I had every right!" he yelled back, "I'm his father!"

"Okay, I have to talk to Chase before I give you my address," she told him.

"I already know where you live," he informed her.

She stared at him in disbelief.

"Like I said, I've done my homework. I'll be in touch," he said as he got into his car. And with that, he was gone as quick as he had come.

Chapter Forty-Three

Things had not been going well. Mekhi didn't take too kindly to Bryce trying to squeeze his way back into Charese's life, especially after he had abandoned her. Charese's mind was already made up. She loved Bryce deeply and they shared a son, a connection she didn't have with Mekhi; yet, she knew that she still wanted to be Mrs. Mekhi Stevens. She had to do what was best for Chase's future and Bryce's track record wasn't good with her.

She was twenty-five now; it was time to grow up. She had to think for not only herself, but her two-year-old son as well. As soon as she told Bryce that she was still marrying Mekhi, he disappeared again. This time it didn't bother her because he had already walked out on her once before so she was not surprised by his actions. She was done with him.

She snapped out of her private thoughts as the limo stopped in front of the church. The chauffeur helped her and her bridesmaids out of the back. They all looked up at the church as Courtni grabbed her hand and squeezed it tight.

"You ready girl?" she asked.

"I'm ready," Charese confirmed.

"Well alrighty then!" Taye exclaimed, "Let's get you married!"

They grabbed their bags then headed inside the church.

Once Charese was ready, she stared at herself in the mirror. She was a nervous wreck.

"You okay girl?" Mekhi's sister asked. She and Taye were her bridesmaids; Courtni was her maid of honor.

"I'm nervous," she admitted.

"It's going to be alright. Every bride gets cold feet right before the wedding," Mrs. Bryson told her as she put the veil over her face. "I was sweating bullets on my wedding day," they embraced.

Charese's wedding was to die for; it was gold and burgundy. Her dress was off white with gold trimming and a long train at the end; her bridesmaids were dressed in burgundy form fitting dresses, and her groomsmen looked dapper in all-white tuxedos with burgundy ties. The Bryson's stood in as her parents. It was bittersweet because this was one of the happiest days of her life and her entire family was dead. Mr. Bryson walked her down the aisle while Mrs. Bryson stayed in the pews. When they reached the front of the church, Mr. Bryson kissed her on the forehead then took a seat beside his wife.

"You're a beautiful bride," he said before he sat down.

Charese was shaking, she was so nervous. Mekhi put his hand on the small of her back and rubbed her gently, trying to calm her nerves. She looked over at her son who was looking GQ smooth in a burgundy three-piece suit with a gold tie, and started to cry. Courtni gave her a Kleenex. You could hear "Aww's" coming from every corner in the church. She looked at Mekhi through tears as he mouthed "I love you." She told him that she loved him too.

"Dearly beloved, we are gathered here today to join this man and this woman in holy matrimony," the reverend started.

Charese drowned him out as she thought of all the events leading up to this very moment. She briefly thought of Bryce.

"If anyone sees just cause why these two should not marry, let them speak now or forever hold their peace." There was silence.

"The rings please... Jonathan Mekhi Stevens, do you take Charese Nicole Shaw to be your lawfully wedded wife? To have and to hold, for richer or poorer, in sickness and in health, til death do you part?" the reverend asked.

He looked deep into her eyes as he slipped the ring on her finger. He choked on his emotions. "I do" he said as a single tear escaped from his eye.

"Charese Nicole Shaw," that was all the Reverend got out before the doors to the church swung open. Bryce shot through the doors like a bat out of hell and ran down the aisle. She looked at Mekhi who looked like he was about to explode.

Bryce completely dismissed Mekhi. "Charese please, I can't let you do this," he said as he took her hand. Mekhi to a step forward, but his best man grabbed him and stopped him.

"Bryce," Charese said.

"No hear me out," he interrupted as he started crying.

She had never seen him cry before.

"I know I fucked up baby. But let me make it right. I promise I will do right by you and Chase. I want to be a family. I'm still in love with you Charese. Please don't marry him," he begged.

She was crying as well as she took his hand in hers, "I love you too Bryce, I do. But I'm in love with Mekhi. There's a difference," she said. She heard Mekhi let out a sigh of relief as Bryce's eyes turned cold.

"Charese please," he begged again.

"I just can't go back to that life," she told him.

"I can't lose you. I couldn't stand it if I lost you forever," he said.

She looked at Mekhi then back to Bryce. She was silent for all of five minutes before she spoke.

"I don't know what to do," she said, shocking everyone in attendance.

"You have to choose Reesy," Mekhi said. "Who is it going to be?"

She stood in the middle of her past and her future.

"I don't know," she said as she picked up her train and ran from the altar.

Courtni and Taye followed right behind her. They were going to have to help their friend fix this mess of hers. She was going to have to choose between Bryce and Mekhi.

Made in the USA
Charleston, SC
03 October 2015